"This is amazing," Jamie said.

On the wall inside the conference center hung poster-size news articles about the Martin family and their philanthropic efforts. "I had no idea your organization funded all of this. You must be very proud."

"We all are," Whit said. "It's funny, but if you had told me in college that I would spend my days giving away the family money, I'd have laughed in your face."

"Didn't your family want you to go into politics?"

"That's one of the chosen Martin paths, yes." He didn't realize he'd told her about it. "But I pretty much blew that plan out of the water my first year in Europe."

"From the looks of things, you landed in precisely the right spot."

Her words warmed him from the inside out. *God, I want to kiss you right now*, he thought.

He settled for a sincere "Thank you. That means a lot."

There was nothing he'd like to do more than bask in her approval. Unfortunately, he knew that wasn't possible. Eventually, they were going to have to talk about what had happened in Europe.

Dear Reader,

I am in love with Whit Martin, the hero of this story. He is so deliciously broken. I won't spoil the story by telling you how. Let's just say that if ever there was a billionaire in need of love, it's Whit. Naturally the only person who can give him the love he needs is the heroine, Jamie Rutkowski.

Reunited with Her Blue-Eyed Billionaire is about choices. When they were lovers at Harvard, Whit and Jamie chose to keep their feelings a secret from one another. Seven years later, they're given a second chance. Will they make the same mistake, or will they let themselves find happiness?

Their journey will take them from Boston to Manhattan. There's a Renaissance museum and a Roman bath, along with a few other romantic adventures.

As I type this, the world is slowly coming out of the coronavirus lockdown. Like most of the world, I spent almost three months unable to travel past my front yard. I have to confess, writing this story helped make a stressful time a little easier. I hope you enjoy reading it. Let me know what you think at Barbara@Barbarawallace.com.

As always, thank you for reading.

Barbara

Reunited with Her Blue-Eyed Billionaire

Barbara Wallace

HARLEQUIN®

Romance™

Recycling programs for this product may not exist in your area.

ISBN-13: 978-1-335-56688-1

Reunited with Her Blue-Eyed Billionaire

Copyright © 2021 by Barbara Wallace

This edition published by arrangement with Harlequin Books S.A.

For questions and comments about the quality of this book, please contact us at CustomerService@Harlequin.com.

Harlequin Enterprises ULC
22 Adelaide St. West, 40th Floor
Toronto, Ontario M5H 4E3, Canada
www.Harlequin.com

Printed in U.S.A.

Barbara Wallace can't remember when she wasn't dreaming up love stories in her head, so writing romances for Harlequin Romance is a dream come true. Happily married to her own Prince Charming, she lives in New England with a house full of empty-nest animals. Occasionally her son comes home, as well! To stay up-to-date on Barbara's news and releases, sign up for her newsletter at barbarawallace.com.

Books by Barbara Wallace

Harlequin Romance

Destination Brides

One Night in Provence

The Men Who Make Christmas

Christmas with Her Millionaire Boss

Royal House of Corinthia

Christmas Baby for the Princess
Winter Wedding for the Prince

The Vineyards of Calanetti

Saved by the CEO

Their Christmas Miracle
Her Convenient Christmas Date
A Year with the Millionaire Next Door

Visit the Author Profile page
at Harlequin.com for more titles.

To Peter, Andrew and Nicole. The best husband and kids a woman could ask for. Stay safe!

To the Sisterwives. Thank you for being there when I needed you.

And finally, thank you to all the great editors and staff at Mills & Boon who made the past eleven years an absolute joy. One of these days I'll be on time.

CHAPTER ONE

THE RENAISSANCE COURTYARD at Boston's Gardner Museum smelled like a rainforest. Orchids of all colors and sizes filled the courtyard, mixing with ferns and pines to create a subtropical paradise. Tucked between a pair of fifteenth-century statues, a harpist added soft notes to the floral tapestry. It was the perfect romantic setting for an engagement party.

Not to mention showing an ex-boyfriend what he'd passed up seven years ago.

Jamie Rutkowski's stiletto heels tapped on the cement as she strode toward the bar. She was a woman on a mission, one that demanded a glass of champagne.

"There you are!" Her best friend and the bride-to-be, Keisha, appeared in front of her, arms spread wide. She wrapped Jamie in a warm hug before stepping back to admire Jamie's outfit. "Look at you all dressed up like a supermodel. You know it's against the rules to outshine the bride at her own engagement party, right?" she said.

"Like I could do that." No one could outshine her fashionista friend, although Jamie was giving it her best shot in a raspberry silk dress that stopped just short of midthigh. Her credit card had wept a little when she bought it, but, Jamie rationalized, you couldn't put a price on revenge.

Keisha, on the other hand, could have worn a sack instead of her designer dress and the happiness on her face would still make her look perfect.

"You look amazing," Jamie said. "Being engaged agrees with you."

"Thank you," her friend replied, "but I'm still putting you in an ugly bridesmaid dress, just in case. Since when do you do the sex kitten thing anyway? I haven't seen you in heels that high in, like, forever. Oh…" Realization broke across her features. "This is all for Whit."

"I don't know what you're talking about." Jamie's attempt at playing innocent failed spectacularly. She and Keisha had been friends far too long.

Her friend looked at her through her false eyelashes. "I'm the one who held your hair back after you drank yourself stupid over the guy, remember."

"Don't be ridiculous. We were over years ago. I've barely given him a thought since graduation." Other than a few Google searches and some Facebook stalking, but innocent curiosity was normal, wasn't it? Everyone looked up their old flames when they'd had a few drinks or suffered a breakup.

"Then why the knockout dress?" Keisha asked.

"Why not? What's wrong with wanting to look like a million bucks for my best friend's engagement party?"

Said best friend gave her a skeptical stare.

"All right," Jamie said reluctantly, "so I wanted to make sure I look really good when I saw him. If you were going to see your ex-boyfriend, wouldn't you want him to appreciate what he'd passed up?"

Every woman had at least one relationship regret, and Whitmore Martin was hers. Handsome, ultra cool and filthy rich, he'd been the dream boyfriend of every girl on their college campus. Jamie had crushed on him for two solid years, never dreaming he'd ever take notice of a no-name scholarship girl like her. But he did notice her, and for an amazing semester and a half, they'd been an item. Until he graduated and took off for Europe, never to be heard from again.

The worst thing was that Jamie couldn't even hold his leaving against him. He'd told her when they'd first got together that he'd signed a contract to play polo in Europe. Because that's what ultra cool, filthy rich guys did when they graduated. Join the professional polo circuit. She was the one who'd agreed to a temporary fling and then proceeded to fall in love with a guy a million miles out of her league. Every time she thought of what a foolish idiot she'd been, it made her cringe.

"What's wrong with making sure that when Whit sees me, he knows I'm successful and living my best life?"

"You don't need a dress for that," Keisha replied. "You've got a fantastic career. How many other people do you know who have had two books hit the bestseller lists?"

"Neither of which had my name on the cover," Jamie pointed out. None of her ghostwritten pieces did. Made bragging about her achievements difficult. "This dress will communicate my winner status without me having to say a word. Then all I have to do is smile dismissively, flip my ponytail and tell him, 'Later.'"

Keisha pursed her smoked purple lips. "A classic passive-aggressive move. I approve."

"What can I say? I've learned from the best," Jamie replied. Keisha waved her off with fake modesty. "Next thing you know, I'll bump into an old classmate while buying sushi and end up engaged too."

"Best sushi I ever had." Keisha smirked.

"Hey, baby, look who decided to make an appearance," said a voice from behind Jamie. It belonged to Keisha's fiancé, Terrance.

"Better get your ponytail ready," Keisha said through a frozen grin. She held out her arms for a hug. "Oh, my God, Whit Martin! Come here, you!"

Jamie stared at the man hugging her friend. Whit had changed since she'd last seen him. There was a worldly air about him now, a kind of seen-it-all sophistication that couldn't be faked. He had a seriousness about him as well, evident by the lines at the edges of his blue eyes and a pair of newly acquired glasses that gave him a sexy professor vibe. Gone too was the windblown crop of golden hair. The new, mature Whit's hair was cropped short and tight. Jamie had a feeling the style might be to partially mask a receding hairline, but that hardly mattered at all. The man still charged the room with his presence.

And Jamie's breath still hitched at the sight of him.

"Keisha, you look incredible. Better than this guy deserves," Whit said.

He then gave Terrance a playful slap on the arm before finally looking at her. "Hey, Jamie." They were the first words he'd said to her since their goodbye seven years ago. To Jaime's own disgust, his soft voice twirled right down her spine. "Good to see you again."

"Good to see you too," she replied. Thankfully she could at least sound indifferent. "How have you been? Are you still living in Europe?" Keisha had already told her that he wasn't, but this way it didn't sound like they'd been talking about him.

"No. I'm based in New York." He answered quickly, as though she'd asked something distasteful, and continued. "That's why I'm late. My last meeting ran long. I finally told them to settle things on their own and got to Boston as quickly as I could."

"Please tell me you took the copter," Terrance said. "I love telling people my buddy's got his own helicopter."

"Technically it's not my own; it belongs to the foundation, but yes, I took the copter."

Nice to see not everything had changed about him. He was still living large. Jamie thought about the last time she'd drunk-surfed the 'net for his picture. It was a few years ago. She remembered finding a bunch of pictures of him in Capri with a pair of beautiful blondes on his arms and champagne bottles in both hands. Clearly loving life.

She forced a little extra brightness into her smile. "See, Keisha, I told you your engagement was a big deal. People are flying in especially for your party."

"How could I not fly in to celebrate your engagement?" Whit asked. "I had to, if for no other reason than to figure out how Terrance managed to get a goddess like Keisha to date him, let alone agree to spend the rest of her life with him."

"I did it totally for the finger bling," Keisha said, before leaning in and tweaking her fiancé's chin. "Just kidding, boo. You know I would have waited forever for you."

They kissed, and Jamie found herself trying not to feel jealous. Across from her, Whit was suddenly interested in his drink. His obvious discomfort helped. Meant she wasn't the only one finding the moment awkward.

Terrance saved them both by speaking. "We should get moving if you want to do this. My mom is asking us to cut the engagement cake."

"Do what?" Jamie asked.

"Kish and I want to get the wedding party together for a toast. I sent everyone down to the Blue Room."

Keisha hooked her arm in Jamie's and started walking toward the doorway on the north side of the garden. "Terrance thought it would be cool to have the toast in the Dutch Room in front of one of those empty frames."

"You mean where the missing paintings hung?" The museum, which had been robbed of nearly a dozen paintings in 1990, continued to display the frames as a way of reminding the public the art had never been recovered.

"What can I say? He's been fascinated by the robbery ever since he read your book. Anyway, I told him that room was way too dark and gloomy, so we compromised. This room is brighter and yet still has one of those creepy empty frames left over from the art theft. Are you okay?" Keisha added the last part in a whisper so the men behind them couldn't hear.

"Fine," Jamie replied. "Why wouldn't I be?" What did she care if Whit didn't act the least bit impressed by her appearance? Shame on her for thinking she was that important a memory. Like she'd ever be memorable to a man who partied with models and had a private helicopter? "If anything, it was anticlimactic. He's just a guy I used to know."

"If you say so," Keisha said doubtfully. "He seems different, don't you think? I know he looks different with his hair so short now, but there's something else too. I can't put my finger on it."

"I know what you mean." Jamie couldn't define the difference either. It was something about his eyes, but she couldn't say exactly what.

As Terrance said, the rest of the wedding party was waiting for them. They stood in a small clump in the center of the room. Over the years, they'd done a lot of socializing, so Jamie knew the bridal party pretty well. They greeted her with hellos and compliments. A similar burst of conversation came from the men in the room upon Whit's entrance. Comments about time passing and hairline jokes rippled through the group.

Stepping back from the crowd, Jamie marveled at the way Whit's presence immediately brought a zing to the atmosphere. He glided more than walked his body teeming with confidence and grace. People's attention was drawn to him like a magnet, not because of his good looks, but because he exuded a superiority that made everyone else in the room fade into the background.

She remembered the first time she saw him on campus. It was a couple weeks into her freshman year and Whit was playing Frisbee outside the residence halls. He had a deep golden tan and sun-streaked hair that stood up on end from his fingers constantly combing through it. She remembered thinking he was the most beautiful boy she'd ever laid eyes on. Make that man. He looked far more sophisticated than any boy from her high school. So beautiful he almost seemed to glow. Now, despite the serious expression behind his designer glasses, the man still glowed, and she was yet again just another girl in the crowd.

She'd worn uncomfortable shoes for nothing.

"Good to have you back, bro."

Whit acknowledged the greeting and good-natured ribbing with a smile he didn't feel. Being back among his college friends was a painful reminder of his former self, a person he wished had never existed. It wasn't his friends' fault. They remembered the past through nostalgia-colored glasses. They didn't know he cringed with shame from any reminder of his former reckless behavior.

A flash of raspberry pink caught his eye. Jamie had separated from the group to stand by an antique desk near the window. She stood with her hands clasped behind her, studying the art hanging on the blue tapestry wall. She looked good, amazing really. In college, she'd been more of a T-shirt and jeans kind of gal. Of course, people changed. God knows, after everything it had been through, his body certainly felt way older than twenty-eight. In Jamie's case, time had definitely worked in her favor. The shimmery pink material draped her body in all the right places, and it'd taken all his self-control not to stare when he first saw her this evening. Last thing he wanted to be was the creepy ex who couldn't let go of the past.

He remembered the first time he'd really noticed her. First semester, senior year. Storytelling through History. He'd only taken the class because he'd needed to fulfill a requirement and had heard the professor was an easy grade. Jamie was an English major. One of those quiet, diligent students who arrived early, sat in the front row and hung on the professor's every word. Whit had stared at the back of her head for two weeks without ever seeing her face.

Then one rainy, blustery day, something had held her up and she'd rushed into class late. Her cheeks were pink from the wind, with strands of damp curls stuck to her cheeks. Whit remembered watching her comb through the wet locks with her fingers and wondering how such a gorgeous face had managed to fly under his radar.

After that, English class got a lot more interesting. Whit had made a point of getting to know her and discovered that diligent facade hid a biting sense of humor. During class discussions, Whit enjoyed pushing her buttons because he knew she'd eventually get frustrated and give him some kind of sarcastic reply, and when their paths had crossed at a party later that semester, he'd done what any red-blooded college senior would do: he'd made his move.

What he'd figured would be a one-night stand had lasted the rest of the college year. Jamie, he'd quickly realized, was prettier, funnier and smarter than most of the girls on campus. Why waste time chasing second best? In fact, he'd almost—almost—suggested they try a long-distance thing, but she'd been so cool about his leaving for Europe that he didn't. "Who says I'm looking for a commitment?" he'd remembered her saying the very first night they'd slept together.

How different his life might have been if he hadn't changed his mind. Looking at Jamie now, it was clear she'd done just fine after he left. He wondered if she ever thought of him like he thought of her, or if he had been relegated to a pleasant but distant memory. His money was on the distant memory.

A server stopped to offer him champagne for the toast. Helping himself to two glasses, he walked over and offered her one. "Can't make a toast without a glass in your hand."

"Thanks."

"My pleasure." He watched her take a sip while letting his own full glass dangle from his fingers. It was a posture he'd perfected over the past few months, having discovered it was easier to hold an untouched drink than stand there empty-handed.

"Can you believe my old roommate is marrying your old roommate?" He nodded toward the couple at the center of the room. "When Terrance told me they were dating, I couldn't believe it."

"I know, right? They ignored each other all through college."

Whit had forgotten the adorable way her eyes crinkled when she smiled. "By the way," he said, "I meant to tell you before. You look great. That dress is amazing on you."

He'd also forgotten how deliciously pink her cheeks got when she blushed. Her long lashes swept over her eyes as she glanced away. "Thank you. You look good too."

That was a lie, but he wouldn't challenge it. Instead, he turned to the wall display, where on the same wall as the portrait of a stern-looking woman, there was a noticeable space.

"A Manet hung there," Jamie said, noting his gaze. Took him a moment to realize she was talking about one of the paintings stolen during the museum's infamous art theft. Perhaps to avoid touching on more personal topics? "The larger one, the portrait, was out for cleaning the night of the break-in," she told him. "Makes you wonder, had it been here, if we'd be looking at another empty frame right now."

Probably. The museum seemed to have immortalized the stolen works by leaving their empty frames hanging on the walls. "I know the stolen paintings are still missing, but don't you think that after three decades, the museum would have purchased a few replacements?"

Jamie shrugged. "As many people come here because of the robbery as they do to see the art. Did you know the whole thing took hardly any time at all? The robbery, I mean. The thieves came in the front door, tied up the security guard, took the Degas works and the Manet from this floor, and then went upstairs to take the three Rembrandts, the Flinck and the Vermeer. They were in and out in just eighty-one minutes."

"That's quite the download of information," he said. More than he'd anticipated.

"Sorry. Force of habit." Her cheeks pinked again. "I wrote a book about the theft."

She'd carried through on her plan after all. Whit felt a bittersweet surge of pride. "Congratulations. You always said you wanted to be a writer. I'm impressed."

One night, while doing homework—well, she'd been doing homework, he'd just been waiting for her to finish so they could get down to more important business—she'd mentioned that she planned to write a novel.

"What's the title? I'd love to read it."

She studied her drink again. "Surprisingly enough, it's called *Eighty-One Minutes*."

"Wait a minute, there's a streaming series named that, isn't there? Is the series based on your book? I thought it was written by some detective." At least that was who was doing the interviews.

"Technically…" She sounded almost sheepish. As though embarrassed. "His name is on the cover, but I wrote the words. I… I ghostwrote it for him," she added, probably because he looked confused.

"Still, you wrote a book," he said. "I couldn't write one." Let alone one that became a television series at that. Whit was truly impressed. From the looks of things, Jamie had gone on to do well for herself. He was glad. Nice to know not everyone had wasted their potential after leaving college.

Happy laughter permeated the room. Correction, Whit realized. *No one else* had wasted their potential.

"Hey," he said, refusing to let the dark mood take hold of him. "Did you ever write that story you talked about? What was it, something about a cursed necklace?"

"An amulet." She looked surprised that he'd remembered it. To be honest, he was too. Recalling pillow talk wasn't exactly his forte when he was younger. Then again, one didn't normally do a lot of talking during a hookup. He and Jamie, on the other hand, had talked a lot. Like had actual grown-up conversations, about life and dreams. Things that mattered. Okay, maybe he hadn't exactly bared his soul to her—as a rule he didn't bare his soul to anyone—but he'd definitely shared more with Jamie than anyone else before or after her. And he'd definitely liked listening to her talk. Her voice had the sweetest cadence.

"Not yet." Her reply brought him back to the present. "I've been working on it, but I have to squeeze in the work between projects and I've been pretty busy lately. I just wrapped up a project for a local investment CEO. And last year I wrote a memoir for a former minor league baseball player about his battle with depression and substance abuse that's being released soon. He talked about everything, warts and all. It was pretty powerful stuff."

"Sounds like it was a hard book to write." Whit looked down at his untouched drink, a burning sensation forming in his sternum.

"Probably not as hard as it was for him to tell the story in the first place. I can't imagine getting trapped in such a downward spiral. Talk about ugly."

She has no idea. "Why put it in a book, then?"

"In this case, the guy, Frankie, is hoping to launch a speaking career where he goes around talking about his experiences and advocating for mental wellness. The hope is for the book to sell well so he can book engagements."

"And if the book doesn't sell?" he asked. "Does he get mad at you?"

"God, I hope not," she said, giving a soft laugh. "If the book doesn't sell, I think Frankie will still be happy. He said doing the project gave him a lot of closure emotionally. What about you? What's Whit Martin doing these days? Last time we saw each other, you were heading to Europe to wave a mallet."

"Only you would refer to polo as 'waving a mallet.'"

"Are you still playing?"

"No. I retired a couple years ago." That wasn't the entire truth, but it was close enough to get by. "I run a charitable foundation these days."

"Really?"

"Surprising, right?" In college, he'd been Mr. Good Times, more interested in having fun than helping others. "When I got back to the States, I wanted to do something that would contribute to society. The Martin family has a tradition of being civilly minded, and goodness knows, there's certainly the need, so I created an organization to support underserved neighborhoods around the country."

"Wow, I'm impressed," Jamie replied.

That made one of them. "Certainly, it's more productive than hitting a ball with a mallet," he said wryly.

A silence fell between them as they stood smiling at one another. Whit struggled to think of something to say. He wasn't ready to end the conversation.

"Hey, you two." Keisha appeared by his side in a flash of purple satin. "I hate to break you up, but we need to get this toast going. Terrance's mother is breathing down my neck about cutting the foolish engagement cake."

"You had me at 'cake,' babe," Jamie said with a smile. "Lead the way." Before Whit could say anything, the two women walked away.

Meanwhile he stayed behind and watched them head to the center of the room, where the rest of their friends had gathered in a circle. Once upon a time, he would have been in the center of the crowd, leading the others in teasing the bride and groom. The life and soul of the party.

Now there were days where he could barely stand to look at himself.

If the therapists at the rehab clinic were here, they would immediately chastise him for the thought, and give him a long speech about self-compassion and forgiveness. *You can't blame yourself for an accident,* they'd say. *Forgive yourself and move on.* They were very good at giving him those speeches. Two years later, he was still trying.

He listened as Terrance toasted his thanks to the bridal party. His former roommate wore a goofy smile that only a man completely head over heels could manage. Keisha's smile matched.

Seeing them left an empty ache in Whit's chest. Would be a long time—if ever—before a woman looked at him with the same besotted expression. Who could love a man with blood on his hands?

A cheer went up and the group raised their glasses before clinking them with one another. Whit lifted his as well, but he was more interested in the woman wearing the raspberry dress standing in front of him. Taking advantage of the commotion around him, Whit let his eyes roam down her figure, remembering the body beneath the dress. The women who'd crossed his path in Europe had nothing on her. Most of them had been fake-breasted toothpicks living on cigarettes and diuretics. Jamie, on the other hand, was athletically built. Lean but muscular, with legs built for straddling a man. She also had a brain. Something else the toothpicks had lacked. Although in fairness to the toothpicks, he hadn't exactly used his own brain all that much in Europe himself.

He really was glad Jamie had found success. *Ghostwriting.* Not quite the career he'd envisioned for her, but he wasn't at all surprised to hear she did it well. If he were to ever want to share his story with the world, she'd be the kind of person he'd pick to work with too. He made a note to buy that baseball player's memoir. The man deserved more than closure for airing his messes. For that matter, could someone even get closure from sharing their story?

Wouldn't that be great, if it were true? he thought. If, by putting all your demons on paper, you could not only help others, but find a way to cleanse your soul?

What if…? Whit watched as Jamie's ponytail bounced in response to her laughter. "Things happen for a reason," the therapists used to say in rehab. "You just have to pay attention to what the universe is trying to say." The therapists had said a lot of woo-woo type stuff. Whit usually ignored them. But what if they had a point? What if the universe was trying to tell him something by dropping Jamie Rutkowski back into his life?

"So, thank you all for joining us for the engagement party, and here's to a terrific wedding," he heard Terrance add. On the other side of the circle, his old roommate raised his glass for a second time. "Cheers." The crowd cheered in return, and everyone began clinking glasses with one another again.

Jamie turned away from the circle, only to duck her head shyly upon seeing him standing behind her. "Cheers," she said.

"To a fun few months," he said, tapping the rim of his still-full glass to hers.

"Hope so. I'll settle for them being drama-free."

"How much drama could there be between now and then? All we have to do is show up on the day and do what we're told."

She eyed him over her glass. "You ever been in a wedding before?"

"A couple, when I was a teenager." Both weddings, if he remembered rightly, were large, formal family-laden affairs and deadly dull. He and the other groomsmen had done a few shots beforehand to get through them. "I don't remember any problems."

"Trust me, there's always drama. Someone's dress doesn't fit, or someone else skips the shower planning meetings or doesn't get the exact shoes the bride requested."

"Makes me glad I'm not a bridesmaid. I am pretty sure groomsmen don't have any of those problems."

"Consider it the hidden misogyny of weddings," Jamie said. She drained the last of her champagne. "Speaking of, I should go see if there are any bridesmaid instructions. Keisha claims she's going to be a low-key bride, but…"

"She's Keisha."

"Exactly." The atmosphere between them, which had been vacillating between comfortable and awkward all evening, slid back into awkwardness. They both looked to their glasses in hopes of finding something to say.

"Well," Jamie said after a couple seconds. "I guess I'll see you in few months. It was good seeing you."

"Before you go… What did you mean when you said the ballplayer thought the book would bring him closure?"

From the way her brows drew together, she obviously thought the question strange. Whit had to admit, the question did sound like it had come out of the blue.

"He—Frankie—said he'd never told anyone

the complete story from beginning to end before," she said. "I got the impression he thought doing so would be like finally and truly coming clean about his mistakes."

"Makes sense." A lot of sense. After all, wasn't confession supposed to be good for the soul? "Did it help? I mean, did he get the closure he wanted?"

She took her time in answering. "Yeah," she said finally, "it did. When we finished, Frankie said that writing the book really helped clarify some things for him. Why do you ask?"

"No reason. Your comment stuck in my head is all."

"Okay." There was still confusion on her face, but she didn't press. "If that's all you wanted, I'll get off. See you around."

"Actually, there's one more thing." He stopped her again.

Maybe he was crazy, but he was also tired of feeling weighed down. So much of what had happened had been swept under the rug. Exposing it to the light of day might be the answer. God knows, he'd tried everything else.

"Are you free for lunch tomorrow?" he asked.

CHAPTER TWO

JAMIE NEARLY FELL off her heels. "Lunch?"

"I'm not flying back until later tomorrow," he continued. "I was hoping we could talk first."

Ever since she'd learned Whit was also in the wedding, she'd been imagining their reunion, and the cool, disinterested way she would regard him. Going to lunch was not part of the plan.

She shook her head. "I don't think…"

"Or breakfast," he quickly added. "Whatever is more convenient for you."

A shiver decidedly didn't pass down her spine as Jamie studied her former boyfriend. This was the moment she tossed her ponytail and left him wanting more.

She rose on her front foot, ready to spin around. Whit stood in his dark suit, drink untouched, with a look of—was it nervous?—expectancy on his face. As though her acceptance really meant something to him. Jamie hadn't counted on sincerity.

"Mornings are my best writing time," she heard herself saying. "I don't go anywhere until after one."

"Then lunch it is. I'm staying at the Mandarin Oriental. Why don't we meet at the restaurant at, say, one thirty?"

When he smiled, it was as if he hadn't aged a bit. The same boyish sparkle that had always made him so irresistible lit up his eyes. The shiver that didn't run down Jamie's spine earlier, didn't run down it again.

"One thirty will be fine."

"Fantastic. I'll see you tomorrow, then. I'm looking forward to it."

"Yeah," Jamie replied. "Me too." She swore her mouth had a mind of its own.

In a perfect display of irony, it was Whit who then turned and walked away, leaving Jamie standing there wondering what she'd done.

"You what?" Grabbing her by the hand, Keisha dragged Jamie into the Spanish cloister. Since the party was ending, the enclave was empty. "What happened to 'He's in the past; I'm over him'?"

"He is. I am," Jamie replied. Her feet hurt more than ever. There was an antique chair in the corner of the room, and she wondered if security would be angry at her sitting down on an exhibit. "We're only having lunch. You make it sound like he asked me to go away for the weekend."

"Well, you are meeting at a hotel."

"To reminisce and catch up, that's all." Jamie fought to keep from rolling her eyes. She had absolutely zero intention of doing anything more. "Frankly, I'm insulted you think I'm that weak."

Her friend folded her arms. "Seriously? Have you forgotten how quickly you tumbled into bed with him the first time?"

"No, I haven't forgotten," Jamie snapped. They'd slept together the very first night. She, the good girl who had only slept with one other person before Whit. "That was also seven years ago. A lot has changed since then." For starters, she wasn't a starry-eyed student who jumped into things heart first anymore. She was smarter, more pragmatic about her relationships. About life in general, in fact.

"What makes you think Whit is interested in anything beyond talking anyway? For all we know he's got a girlfriend back in New York." Some beautiful woman with an equally old monied name as his. The thought briefly tasted sour in her mouth.

"What if he doesn't? Have a girlfriend?" Keisha asked.

"Then still nothing."

"Are you sure?"

"Positive. This is a revenge dress, remember, not a get-him-back dress." Once upon a time, she might have been foolish enough to think she and Whit had a future together, but that, like so many of her dreams, had been illusory.

In retrospect, it was surprising their affair had lasted as long as it did. She was never in Whit's league. Those photos of him she'd seen online proved it. He went to Europe and never gave her a second thought.

"Besides," Jamie continued, "he's changed since college, don't you think? There's something different about him."

"It's called nearsightedness."

"Ha-ha, I'm not talking about the glasses." Which he rocked anyway. "I'm talking about his demeanor. He's far more serious. Did you know he's running a foundation to help underserved communities?"

"Get out. Terrance just said Whit was working for the family business, so I figured it was some kind of cushy, made-up job. I mean, it's not like the guy ever has to work."

No kidding. Certainly didn't jibe with the man double-fisting bottles of Cristal that she'd seen online. Or, the Whit she knew in college, for that matter.

"He said he wants to contribute to society," she told Keisha.

"Huh," said Keisha. "Goes to show even rich party boys can change."

And change drastically, thought Jamie.

She supposed Whit could have simply grown up—people did, after all, but her gut said there was more to the story. There was a shadow be-hind his eyes that wasn't there before, a serious-

ness that outpaced his years even when he smiled.
There was weariness there too, as though he'd
seen too much of the world. It had flashed across
his face when they were talking about Frankie's
memoir. Those kinds of characteristics didn't just
appear in someone's personality by themselves;
life put them there. How?

"Maybe he'll tell me more over lunch," she said
thoughtfully, earning a hefty sigh from Keisha.

"Guess that means you're going then. Promise
me you won't do something stupid and make the
wedding all awkward, okay?"

"Heaven forbid we cause a problem for the
wedding. Don't worry," she said before Keisha
could speak. "After lunch tomorrow, Whit will
be out of the picture until the wedding."

The hotel bistro was filled with diners and lushly
decorated in shades of maroon with brass trim.
The room's back wall was a greenhouse window
that looked outside onto the street and the Boston
Public Gardens. The midday sun shone through
the glass, making the room feel airy and bright.
Sitting at a corner table, Whit watched the doorway for Jamie's arrival. Underneath the table his
knee bounced up and down, the sole indication
that his insides were a bundle of uncertainty.

Last night's great idea sounded insane in the
light of day. Sharing Martin family skeletons. He

imagined five generations worth of heads exploding at the very thought, with his grandfather's exploding twice for good measure. Right after he finished moralizing at Whit about the need for discretion and maintaining the precious family reputation. Making sure, of course, to note how Whit had already failed the family, despite all his efforts to mold him into a proper Martin.

In other words, a Martin in Grandfather's image and scandal-free. Whit could care less about either. He was never going to be his grandfather, and no family was ever scandal-free. The only difference between his scandals and those of other families was that Whit's were buried deeper than most.

It wasn't angering his family that worried him. It was Jamie. Their relationship was one of the only good memories he had. A sliver of time he could pull from his pocket when things were at their darkest. Preserving that memory was one of the reasons he hadn't contacted Jamie upon returning from Europe. Was gaining closure worth ruining it now? When she learned what had happened in Capri, she'd never look at him the same way again. Whit wasn't sure he could stomach her looking at him with disgust and condemnation.

He'd have to make up his mind quick because at that moment, Jamie walked into the restaurant. She was dressed far more conservatively today.

No more bright pink silk and rhinestone cuffs. Instead she wore a black-and-white-print dress that tied in a bow at her waist. Her hair was in another ponytail, although this one was softer, clasped at the nape of her neck instead of pulled high on her head. Whit sucked in his breath. This was the Jamie he remembered. Beautiful but unassuming. He was surprised heads didn't turn when she walked in the room.

He stood to greet her as she approached the table. "Right on time," he said. "Some things never change."

"And some things do," she replied with a smile. "Seeing as you're on time too."

Whit grinned in return. The woman had a point. He started to lean in to kiss her cheek, but Jamie took her seat before he could. To cover the slight awkwardness, he put his hand on the back of her chair, pretending that was his intention all along.

"What can I say, I've evolved," he told her. "Plus, I only had to take the elevator down three floors."

"You have evolved. There was a time when you couldn't make it across the hall on time."

"Hey, not my fault I kept getting stopped by people to talk," he said as he sat down.

"You know that's the same excuse you always gave in college, right?"

"Points for me for being consistent then." Tossing quips back and forth reminded him of the old days. When she wanted to, Jamie could have a sharp tongue. Whit felt the tension in his shoulders ease. He leaned back in his chair. "I'm glad you came. To be honest, I half expected you to call this morning to say you changed your mind."

"To be honest, I almost did," she replied.

"What made you come, then?"

"I decided I was being silly. We're both mature adults. There's no reason why you and I can't enjoy a meal together. Plus, I've always wanted to eat here. The view of the Public Gardens is really pretty."

Jamie smoothed the napkin on her lap, then straightened the place setting. When she was finished, she reached for her water glass. As he watched her drink, Whit remembered how her hands always had to be in motion. Her long fingers were always touching or fiddling with something. During the first meal they'd shared, he'd teased her about peeling a beer label to shreds.

"Wow," he mused aloud. "Has it really been seven years?"

"Hard to believe, isn't it? Guess it's true, what they say. Time flies when you're having fun."

"Were you? Having fun?"

"More or less." She reached for her water again.

"Glad to hear it. Would it be rude to ask if

there's someone special in your life?" It *was* rude, he thought in retrospect. Her love life was none of his business. He was really curious though. What kind of men did she date? Probably creative, romantic types who treated her to sunset picnics on the beach.

Jamie had hidden her face behind the menu, making it difficult to gauge how she felt about his question. "There've been people," she said. "No one special at the moment."

"Good," Whit replied. He loosened his grip on the napkin he didn't realize he'd been crushing in his fist. "That is, I wouldn't want our having lunch to complicate things for you."

"It won't complicate anything. I am much more focused on my career than dating right now."

"I remember you saying something similar to me seven years ago." When he'd told her he was moving to Europe. "You know what's funny? Before I knew you, when I used to listen to you in class, I would have bet money on you being the romantic type."

"Nope," she said, her face still hidden. "Romance is unrealistic as far as I'm concerned."

"So you always said." Something about her voice sounded odd. Tight maybe. If only the menu wasn't blocking her face. He would have liked to have seen her expression.

Something else he noticed. She didn't ask him

if he had a significant other. Either she assumed he didn't or, more likely, she didn't care if he did or not. His ego took a little hit at the thought.

At that moment, the waitress returned with their drinks and to take their orders. By the time Whit had selected his flavor of tea and they'd gone through the specials, the moment for asking had passed.

"Tea, huh?" Jaime noted as he unwrapped his Earl Grey. "What happened to the guy who mainlined coffee?"

"Oh, he's still around. I've learned to mix things up a bit since my return. Become multifaceted as it were."

"You've also started to use words like *multifaceted*," she said. "Arriving on time, tea, expanded vocabulary. You have definitely evolved, Whitmore."

"You make it sound like I was uncivilized in college. You're forgetting all my good qualities."

"No, I'm not. But I can't tease you about those."

She shot him a smile from over her wineglass. Whit had no choice but to smile back as he filled his teacup with pale amber liquid. The tea wasn't quite steeped enough, but he was too impatient.

"Tell me more about this foundation of yours," she said. "I thought your family already had a foundation."

"They had two. One for the arts, one for science and technology. But they're already run by family members. I wanted to focus on programs that are more socially oriented and have control over the process."

"So you created a third."

"It was either that or get an honest job," he replied with a grin.

"Plus, you get to make a difference."

His smile faded. "Yeah, I do." The honest job line was one he used often. Not only did it draw chuckles, but it kept people from digging any deeper into his motivations. He hadn't expected Jamie to recount his own words from last night.

"Anyway, we're focusing on substance abuse and mental health initiatives. This past year we conducted research into the economic impact of these issues on underserved communities. Our plan is to establish a nationwide program that will provide not only affordable treatment but also financial support to the affected families."

"Sounds like a huge undertaking. If it were me, I'm not sure I'd even know where to start. I'd be overwhelmed."

"Trust me, I was in the beginning. It helps to put together a top-notch staff." What he didn't say was how the research and groundwork had amplified his personal shame and that there were days when it took all his strength not to jump back into the abyss with the rest of the addicts and alcoholics.

"Well, I have to admit, I'm impressed," she said.

Don't be; I don't deserve praise. "Don't you mean surprised?" he asked.

She shook her head. "I—"

"It's all right. I'm not insulted." They both knew how directionless he'd been in college, content to just float along in life. After all, it'd worked for his father.

"Well, it is a big jump from professional polo player. Which, when I say it out loud, also sounds impressive."

"Hardly. I only signed on because it was an excuse to ride every day." As well as avoid whatever it was his grandfather wanted him to do. "The job isn't nearly as glamorous as it sounds."

"Still beats my first job out of college. I waited tables full time. Remember Sabrosa?"

"The Mexican place. Sure. I remember we used to sit at your table and drink margaritas all night."

"You always left me a generous tip," she said.

"You always got mad at me for it," he shot back.

"Because I didn't want you to think I was with you for the money."

"Why would I think that?"

"Isn't it obvious?" Picking up a fork, she twisted the handle between her fingers. "I mean, I was a scholarship kid and you were…"

"Rich?"

"Richer than rich," she replied. "I heard the way girls talked about you. You were the biggest catch on campus. Everyone wanted to be the girl who snagged you."

He raised an eyebrow. "You make me sound like a prize fish."

"Maybe not a fish, but definitely a prize. You'd be surprised how many women have a secret Cinderella fantasy. Marry the billionaire and live a life of wealth and privilege."

"But not you."

"I didn't care about wealth and privilege," she said flatly as she tapped the fork's tines on the tablecloth. "Besides, everyone knows Cinderella is a work of fiction."

Something about her answer unsettled him but he couldn't say what. Perhaps it was the assumption he was Prince Charming in that scenario. An idea even more ludicrous than her being Cinderella.

"For what it's worth, I never thought you were after my money. Never once."

He looked across the table. Her eyes were more beautiful than he remembered. Cocoa brown with flecks that turned golden in the light. He bet a person could stare into them a thousand times and never stop discovering something new. Like the way dark lines spread from her pupils like a starburst.

Someone cleared their throat. Whit sat back in his chair just in time for their meals to be served. They spent the lunch sharing college memories and exchanging updates about the few classmates they both knew. The conversation came easy, as did the laughs. Sitting in the sunshine, sharing a chocolate torte, Whit almost forgot the reason he'd invited Jamie to lunch.

Almost. His mission came as the waitress brought over a second pot of hot water. Washing down his final bite of torte, he eased into the subject. "By the way, I downloaded your art theft book and read some of it last night."

"Really?"

"You sound surprised."

"I am, a little," she replied.

"You shouldn't be. It's not every day a friend writes a book. I really enjoyed it."

The real reason, of course, was that he wanted to sample her work before they talked. Having read her papers back in school, he knew she could write. What surprised him was how the book sounded exactly like it had been written by a gruff, retired police detective.

"Do your books always sound like the people who hired you?" he asked.

"As much as possible, they do. Fortunately, a

lot of what I write are business books. With those I can get away with letting my own voice creep in a bit more."

"That must take some skill."

"My agent thinks so," she replied. He waited while she ate the piece of torte she'd sliced off. Her clients probably loved working with her, he imagined. She was easy to talk to and easy to look at. A sexist opinion, yes, but he refused to take back the compliment.

"How did you get involved in writing other people's books?" he asked her. "I'm guessing you didn't wake up one morning and say, 'I'm going to be a ghostwriter.'"

She shook her head. "Honestly? I fell into it. I was working for a small company and one of our clients needed someone to edit a book she'd written. Long story short, the manuscript sucked, and I ended up rewriting the whole thing, saving the client a ton of embarrassment. A year later I signed on with a ghostwriting agency, learned I could make way more money and be my own boss, and voilà. A career is born."

"And that book by the ballplayer you told me about. Was that something your agent arranged?"

"Yeah, it was…" She set down her fork and looked at him straight on. "Why do you sound like you're giving me a job interview? Are you looking to write a book?"

"Actually…" Did he really want to do this? There was still time to change his mind. He could make up some lame excuse and forget all about telling his story.

And then what? He needed this monkey off his back once and for all, and if he could help someone else in the process, then so be it.

If he was going to expose his skeletons, however—he signaled the waitress—he needed black coffee rather than tea.

Jamie was waiting for him to continue. With a deep breath, he plowed forward. "Actually, I want you to write a story. A cautionary tale about a man's descent into booze, drugs and destruction and the damage he left behind."

"Who…?"

The question faded off. Whit saw in her eyes the moment her brain answered her own question. She knew, but she was afraid to say so out loud. He said it for her. "Me, Jamie. I want you to tell my story."

Jamie blinked. She heard Whit's words, but they didn't sound right. How could the man sitting across from her, with his Brooks Brothers jacket and his preppy little glasses, the man she'd made love with for several months, how could he be an addict? Had that much changed in seven years? "I don't understand," she told him. "How?"

"How else? I got sucked in." The rest of his

answer had to wait as the waitress poured their coffee. Damn woman seemed to be hovering the entire meal.

"That's the thing about addiction. It sneaks up on you," he said once she'd left. "You think you have everything under control until you wake up one day and realize addiction has control of you. I spent six months in a clinic in Switzerland getting clean before I returned to New York."

This was unreal. Even after they broke up, Whit had been someone she considered a plane above, his only flaw being that he didn't love her.

She looked down at the crumbs left from her chocolate torte. Tiny dark pieces scattered across white porcelain where a gorgeous dessert once sat. Staring at them, she had the strange and sudden urge to piece them back together. Impossible since the torte was gone, but that didn't stop her from wanting to return the bits to their former glory.

"I'm sorry," she said.

"For what? You didn't do anything," Whit replied. "Everything I did, I did all by myself. For better or worse."

He looked away when saying the last part, but not before Jamie caught the intense emotion in his expression. The casual observer wouldn't see it. To most people, Whit looked the picture of control. But she knew Whit's face. The calm was all a front.

"There's more to this story, isn't there?" she asked.

"Of course. The road to sobriety is never pretty. That's why I want to write this book," he told her. "When you told me about that baseball player and how he wanted to use his story to help people, it made me realize I should do the same. People need to know no matter how rich, no matter how famous your last name, you're still going to crash and burn. Bad things will happen."

Suddenly she understood why Whit was so interested in closure.

Although she didn't really want coffee, she took a sip anyway. Ironically, it was the only thing she could think of to keep her nerves in check.

"Am I crazy?" Whit asked. "Is it a stupid idea?"

"Not at all." The Martins were American royalty. Whit's name on the cover would guarantee publication and publicity. "It's just that, a book is a very public way of sharing your story." And Whit, for all his congeniality, was a very private person. As she'd learned the hard way, he liked to keep people at arm's length. "If you want this memoir to really make a difference," which he said he did, "then you're going to have to be brutally honest and share a lot of uncomfortable details."

"I know."

"What about your family? Are they okay with this?"

"My family will have to deal with it." There was a chilly edge to his voice that surprised her. She'd never heard Whit speak so harshly. Why was he now? The answer, she supposed, would come out during the interviews.

That is, if she took on the project. There was still one other, obvious issue to mention. "Are you sure I'm really the best person to write this story?"

"What are you talking about?" His coffee cup rattled in its saucer. "You're the perfect person to do it."

"Am I?" Jamie wasn't so sure. "We have a history, Whit."

"So?"

"So, writing a book like this means spending a lot of time together. Meetings. A least a week of interviews."

"I think we're both capable of being professional. Weren't you saying an hour ago that we are both mature adults?"

Yes, but she'd been referring to having lunch together. Ghostwriting his memoir was entirely different. Did she really want to spend day after day working intimately with the man who'd broken her heart?

"I don't know," she said dubiously.

"Please, Jamie. This is going to be hard enough for me to do. I don't want to talk about it with some stranger. I want someone I can trust." He reached across the table and grabbed her hand. "I want you."

There was a time when she would have done anything to hear Whit say those words. Jamie looked down at the hand holding hers. He was fighting the urge to squeeze tight. The tension showed in the way the skin stretched across his knuckles. She could feel the warmth rising from his skin, the comforting presence seeping through the back of her hand and into her bones. One simple touch shouldn't affect her like this, she thought. But then, how many men had touched her after confessing to a drug addiction? No doubt that was the reason she could feel her pulse beating on her wrist. "Well?" he asked.

She looked up, instantly regretting it when she found herself gazing into eyes the color of a September sky. Damn it. She never could say no to him. "We need to hash out a few business details first." She slid her fingers out from under his. Without Whit's hand on hers she could think more clearly. "You don't just whip out a book. There's a formal process. Contracts to be signed. I'll have to work out the hours and talk to my agent. Make sure she knows I've taken on the project."

"Whatever you need."

Once more, he took her hand. This time his grip was gentle, and his voice laced with relief. "Thank you," he said. "You have no idea how much this means to me."

Actually, thought Jamie, she thought she did. It was the desperation in his eyes that finally convinced her to say yes.

She only wished she didn't regret the decision.

CHAPTER THREE

A WEEK LATER found Jamie sitting at the head of a conference table in one of the Boston Public Library's private conference rooms, waiting for Whit to arrive for their first interview. The page of her notepad was covered with tiny blue dots from her tapping her pen against it. Tap, tap, tap.

Why was she feeling so antsy? It was just an interview. She'd done a lot of interviews. There was no reason for her stomach to feel squirrelly.

Pushing the pad and pen aside, she looked around the room. The space was part of the library's recent renovations, meaning it was sleek and modern in comparison with the main building. Despite this, the air managed to retain the same musty smell that permeated the old collection. She wondered if that was by design or by accident. Either way, the smell was comforting. It reminded her of her hometown library, which was an old mansion with a marble staircase and glossy wood rails. The town was always talking about modernizing the building, but every year, they cut the line item in favor of something else. How she'd loved that library. Whenever the noise from her mother's day care business grew too loud at home, she'd go there to escape. She'd sit at one of the tables, fantasizing that the reading room was her private study and that she was researching her next great novel.

She'd had the whole dream worked out. Scholarship to Harvard, followed by a cute little brownstone apartment on Comm Ave. She'd fall in love with Prince Charming and he'd whisk her away to Paris where she'd drink café au lait and write the great American novel.

By age twenty, she'd found her Prince Charming. Of course, she'd played it cool—Whit was very up front about not wanting a serious relationship—but that didn't stop her heart from tumbling. It was, she'd thought naively, only a matter of time before Whit fell in love with her too.

By age twenty-one Prince Charming had gone to France without her, and she'd pulled her head out of the clouds. Romantic fantasies were just that, fantasies. Better to put her energy into blood, sweat and tears. Dreams were set aside in favor of more practical, achievable goals, like building a career and a healthy bank account. If she ever caught herself daydreaming, she quickly squashed the thoughts and got back to work.

"Don't say a word. It's not my fault." Whit burst through the glass door, his face pink from the cold. He was in preppy mode. Pea coat, peach oxford shirt and khaki trousers. "Landing strip was backed up so the copter had to circle a couple times before we could get down."

He tossed his jacket onto the table and flopped into the seat across from her. "The traffic here was as bad as in New York. I finally had my driver let me off and I walked the rest of the way."

He pulled a water bottle from his briefcase. "Give me a second to catch my breath and I'll be ready to go."

"Take all the time you need. We've got the room for the afternoon." Watching him guzzle his drink, Jamie found herself mesmerized by the way the cords in his neck flexed and relaxed as he swallowed down the contents. Now that she thought about it, the room was little warm. The library must have upped the heat to compensate for the cold weather.

"Ah, much better," Whit said when he finished. "Now I'm ready to function. How are you? Did you get the paperwork I signed and sent back?"

"I did. Thanks for being so prompt."

"I don't believe in leaving paperwork lying around," he replied. "Contrary to today's appearance, I believe in efficiency." He tossed the empty bottle at a nearby wastebasket. It bounced off the wall and landed on the floor next to the container. "Damn, I'm losing my touch."

"Did you ever have one?"

"I liked to think so." The way he looked at her made her insides grow warm.

"You know what?" she said, jumping to her feet, "I'm going to prop the door open so the air can circulate. Then we can begin."

"What exactly are we going to 'begin' doing?" Whit asked.

Jamie was busy wedging a doorstop underneath the glass door. When she returned, she made a point of moving to a seat across the table. For space.

"Today is about getting a broad picture of your story so I can pull together a basic outline for the book. Once we agree on the overall theme, structure and whatnot, then we'll do the in-depth interviews."

"Meaning I won't be baring my soul to you quite yet." Jamie couldn't tell if he was relieved or disappointed.

"More like previewing the soul-baring," she said. "I'm going to ask some general questions and we'll go from there." Reaching into her bag, she pulled out the microphone attachment for her phone. "I hope you don't mind, but I'm going to record all of our meetings. That way I can refer back to them for accuracy."

"Come on, tell the truth now. You want to be able to listen to my voice when you're falling asleep at night."

"Damn, you caught me." The corners of her mouth twitched as she tried not to smile. They were supposed to be acting professionally. She considered asking him if he was this cheeky with everyone he worked with, but she didn't want to know the answer. A no might make her think he was flirting. A yes, on the other hand, would mean she wasn't all that special. She didn't know which answer would affect her more. "First question. How old were you when you had your first experience with drugs or alcohol?"

"Twelve. No, make that eleven and a half. My cousin Monty and I stole a bottle of champagne during a family party in the Hamptons."

Seriously? Jamie's eyebrows shot up. "Whose idea was that?" she asked.

"Probably Monty's, although I'm sure I didn't need too much encouragement. We were always getting into things we shouldn't."

Whit leaned back in his chair with his hands folded across his chest. Beneath the table, his leg was bouncing. She could tell from the way his chair moved. He launched into a long story that involved him and his cousin escaping the nanny's watch and climbing the roof to look for pirate ships when they were eight. He talked with his hands and as the story unfolded, the gestures became more and more animated. Jamie found herself smiling at the image of an eight-year-old

Whit getting into mischief. She wished she knew him then; he sounded adorable. *See if he'll get you a photograph*, she wrote on the top of the paper. For the book. It would make a good visual.

Much as she didn't want to, she steered the conversation back on topic. "Pirate hunting aged eight, champagne stealing at eleven. What happened?"

"What do you think? We hid in the backyard and took turns drinking from the bottle."

"How'd you get the cork out?"

"Fortunately, we'd watched our parents open enough bottles that we had a rough idea." He chuckled. "Damn cork barely missed my head when Monty popped it. Anyway, we drank the half the bottle and then spent the rest of the night puking our guts out. Our parents were not amused."

"I can imagine," Jamie replied. "My parents would have skinned me alive if I'd gotten drunk in middle school."

"My parents were more annoyed that we wasted a two-hundred-and-fifty-dollar bottle of champagne. My father didn't believe in wasting the good stuff. My parents weren't super hands-on, if you get my drift."

Jamie thought of her mother who, even when exhausted from chasing other people's kids around, had always found the energy to sit and watch animated princess movies with her. "If not hands-on, what were they?" she asked him.

He shrugged. "Rich. Sporty. They hosted a lot of parties for artists. My dad considers himself a patron of the arts. They play a lot of tennis too."

That wasn't the most loving description Jamie had ever heard. She tried to remember if she and Whit had ever talked about their families in college. Only in the vaguest of terms, she realized.

On the opposite side of the table, Whit was rocking back and forth in his chair, his expression that of a man focused on the past. "My grandfather," he was saying. "Now, there was a man with very specific ways of child rearing. Specific schools, specific fields of study. Andover prep for the boys, Abbot for the girls, then on to a top university." He paused to pick at the molded arm on his chair. "You would have thought he'd have revised his plan since it didn't work for his own offspring."

"Does everyone do what he says?"

"His sons do. I've recently decided to become a thorn in his side," Whit said with a smirk. "Unintentional consequence of rehab was learning to be my own man and do my own thing."

Like write his memoir. Jamie remembered the emphatic way he'd insisted his family's approval didn't matter. "What you're saying is that you've become a man in charge of your own destiny."

"Why not? Letting someone else run my life sure as hell wasn't working. If the old man wants to disown me for it, let him." Interestingly, his voice was calm and even when he spoke, the way you'd expect a man in charge to speak. Suddenly Jamie recognized the energy she was picking up off him. He'd always radiated confidence, but there had been a youthful cockiness to it. This was the self-assuredness of a man focused and in control. It was incredibly attractive. Way more so than golden hair and a tan. If good ole Grandpa Martin didn't view his grandson with respect, then he was a fool.

"So off you went to Andover," she said. "Where, let me guess, you were king of the cool kids."

The tiniest bit of red spread along his cheekbones. "I did all right. Being Monty's cousin helped. He started the year before me and paved the way."

"Somehow I don't think you needed your cousin to do that."

"You'd be surprised," Whit replied. "I was a lot shyer in my younger years."

Jamie snorted. "Puh-lease. You forget, I've seen your shy side. It's about as shy as a billboard."

"I said when I was younger. I eventually grew out of it."

"When?"

"Around the time I hit six feet and my skin cleared up."

In other words, when he physically developed. She could just imagine Whit returning to school in the fall having blossomed into…well, Whit. All-boys school or not, she could picture everyone on campus wishing they were him. "I should have guessed," she muttered while writing a reminder to herself to ask for his yearbook.

"Hey, like you should talk," Whit replied. "Someone who looks like you? Are you going to tell me you weren't part of the popular crowd?"

Someone who looks like you. Jamie tried not to react to his compliment, but her ego smiled anyway.

"Not really," she replied. "I belonged to a lot of clubs and stuff, but that was to bulk up my extracurriculars. The popular kids didn't really socialize with me." They'd considered her too studious and geeky. Getting good grades was one thing but hanging in the library studying for hours on end was another.

"Wow. Color me shocked."

She wrinkled her nose at his remark. "Do you remember what I was like in college? It took two years for you to even know I existed. What on earth makes you think I would be popular in high school?"

"I don't know. I assumed you were popular by

association because all the cool boys wanted to date you."

"Nope."

"Why not? Were they all stupid?"

Jamie looked away certain she was blushing from head to toe. It wasn't as if a man hadn't called her beautiful before. For goodness' sake, it wasn't even the first time Whit had told her. What was it about Whit's compliments that made her feel like a swan being noticed for the very first time?

"You assume I wanted to be popular," she said, pleased with the amount of nonchalance she managed to inject into her voice. "I was more of a fringe person."

"Striking a pose next to the bar. I remember."

She remembered too. She'd been standing on the sidelines of a frat party when Whit had surprised her by joining her. Leaning shoulder to shoulder against a bookcase, loud music pulsing around them, they'd talked about class, or rather hollered in each other's ears. Throughout the conversation, Jamie had kept expecting him to walk away. Instead, after they'd emptied their red Solo cups, Whit had leaned in and asked if she wanted to grab something to eat.

Jamie still remembered how even in the darkened room, his eyes had looked so bright. How staring into them had set off an unfamiliar but aching need deep inside her. At that moment, she would have gone anywhere he asked. It was no surprise she'd ended up in his bed that night.

She cleared her throat. They were getting off track again. "You said you had your first drink at eleven. Did you keep drinking after that?"

"No, not for a few years," he told her. "In high school, I did." A smile played with appearing as he remembered. "Monty was definitely an influence. Boy knew how to throw a good party."

Monty sounded like a problem child to her, but she kept her opinion to herself. Instead, she asked Whit if any parties were more memorable than others.

For the next two hours, Whit talked about various parties he'd thrown or attended in his teen years. Most of them had the same theme: rich kids getting as messed up as possible. Two things stuck out to Jamie. The first was how absent Whit's parents seemed to be from his life. Almost all his stories involved his being at school or his parents out of town.

The second thing she noticed was more subtle. Actually, it wasn't a thing at all, but rather a realization that Whit, for all his popularity, was largely alone as a child.

"Were you lonely?" She blurted out the question in the middle of another story. "Growing up, I mean. Were you often lonely?"

Whit gave her a crooked look. "What are you talking about? Haven't you been listening for the last couple of hours? I had lots of friends."

"I know, but people can still be lonely in a crowd. Were you?"

He didn't answer. His face shifted into a frown as he looked down at the table. "I made a point of keeping busy," he said finally.

He'd been that way when they were dating too. Always on the move, hopping from one social event to another. Jamie remembered being jealous that she'd had to share his time with others, although she'd never said so. The price of dating the king of the campus, she used to tell herself. But was it the truth? Or had he stayed so busy to avoid being alone? Her heart broke at the thought.

"What?" Whit's voice reached across the table. "You got a sad look on your face all of a sudden," he said.

"Sorry. Just thinking about how to use this information," she lied. She scribbled the word *lonely* with a question mark at the bottom of page as a reminder to revisit the topic. First, she needed to reconcile the idea with the Whit she remembered. To make sure she wasn't projecting an emotion onto him that actually didn't exist.

"You didn't mention your cousin, Monty, in the last story. Was he already away at college?"

"No, he um…" His eyes clouded over as he

suddenly pushed himself away from the table. Jamie's first instinct was to follow him, but she forced herself to stay seated, like she would during any other interview. Instead, it was her eyes that followed Whit to the whiteboard hanging on the wall. "Monty died in a car accident the summer he turned eighteen. Drunk driver crossed the yellow line and struck him head-on."

"I'm so sorry." The ache in her heart magnified.

"Yeah, me too. Guess all those years of partying caught up to him."

"Except this time, it was someone else's drinking that caused the damage." Seemed to her like the ultimate in cruel ironies.

"So the story goes," Whit replied, his voice flat. "I killed a bottle of champagne the night of his funeral. Seemed only fitting." He looked at her from over his shoulder. "Do you mind if we call it a day? My throat is getting dry. I could use a drink."

But they'd only scratched the surface of the things she wanted to cover. Then again, if Whit had mentally checked out, they wouldn't get much more of use anyway. Jamie glanced at the time on her phone. "Sure. I'll see what I can do with the information you've given me. I'll expand the outline after we talk about Europe."

"Good old Europe. I can't wait."

Jamie set down her pen. It hurt to hear the self-recrimination hiding behind the sarcasm. Whatever had happened to him, whatever the reason he needed to seek closure, was more painful than she'd realized. "We're still early in the process," she reminded him. "If you don't want to—"

"No, I do. Want to. I'll be fine. Now pack up your things and let's get something to drink," he said, clapping his hands together.

Jamie pretended not to notice how forced his smile was.

Whit watched while Jamie packed up her materials. She was disappointed that he wanted to stop. The way she hesitated before answering said as much. Today was nothing, he wanted to tell her. Wait until they started talking about Capri. Then she'd really be disappointed in him.

"I can see why you're successful," he told her. "You're a good interviewer."

"I've had a couple years to practice," she replied as she wrapped her phone cord into a coil. "You should have heard me during my first interview. I'm not sure who was more monosyllabic, me or the client."

"I'm going to go with neither." Something he'd noticed over their last few meetings was that she'd developed a warm, natural presence that encouraged people to talk. It was a gift. One he'd never taken full advantage of when they were dating. While she would talk of writing and wax poetic about anything and everything, he'd always held a piece of himself back. Kept his darker side tucked away lest she see the empty, unlovable spots inside him.

Now, however, she'd honed that natural ability into a real skill. Whit could tell by her expression that she wasn't just asking questions, she was *listening*. Her interest in her subject was infused with sincerity. You could see it in the way her eyes mirrored the emotion of the moment. They shone during the happy stories and showed pain during the sad ones. Without realizing, she'd gotten him—who made a point of never sharing—to let down his guard and tell the unblemished truth.

He was going to hate it when the look turned to disappointment.

"There's a café on the first floor," she said. "We can grab a coffee there."

He didn't want to grab anything on the way out. Out meant leaving, and he wanted to enjoy Jamie's company a little while longer. "Actually, I was thinking of somewhere a little quieter," he said.

"We're in a library. How much quieter do you need?"

"Some place that serves more than coffee and day-old muffins," he said. "Didn't I see a sign near the front door advertising something called the Map Room?"

"The new library cocktail bar. It's one of Boston's new trendy places."

A bar in a library. Why not? The Bryant Park library had a café. "Do they serve food?"

Jamie lifted her shoulders. "I assume so."

"Great. We'll go there."

"Oh. Um…" She sounded surprised. "When you asked about getting something to drink, I thought you meant by yourself."

"Now, why would you think that?"

"I don't know. Maybe because you have a helicopter to catch?"

He watched as she played with the clasp on her tote bag, twisting the swivel head back and forth. It was fascinating to see how nimbly her fingers moved when she fidgeted. "You forget, I own the helicopter. Takeoff time is up to me," he said.

She smiled.

"Come on," he urged, drawing closer. Reaching out, he slipped the tote bag from her shoulder. "Don't make me sit by myself drinking tea in the hip new library bar. Let me treat you to an early dinner."

"All right," she said. "But only for a little while. I promised Keisha I'd try on my bridesmaid dress tonight."

Smiling, Whit slipped her bag on his shoulder. "One drink and we're out, I promise."

In years gone by, the Map Room had been exactly that, a room that held rare and antique maps. Now, replicas of the maps adorned the walls while windows in the domed brick ceiling let in light. The old books and Edison-style lightbulbs gave the space a very rustic and cozy atmosphere. The moment they stepped inside the café, Whit knew he liked it.

He liked his company too. Looking to his left, he stole a look at her. During the interview, she'd pulled her hair into a messy topknot. A few loose tendrils had managed to escape and hung around her face. One dangled near her eye, and Whit had the urge to reach over and tuck the strand behind her ear.

Once upon a time, he would have followed through on his urge. Jamie was as desirable as ever, more so really with her added confidence. Whit would be lying if he said he didn't find her massively attractive or wonder if she still kissed as sweetly.

Wasn't it funny that kissing was what he remembered most about being with Jamie? He'd partied and slept with a lot of women. Some had done some crazy stuff in bed. But it was only

Jamie he associated with kissing. Long, slow, incredibly sweet kisses.

"You got awful quiet all of a sudden," Jamie said as they took a seat at one of the wooden tables. "Everything all right?"

He coughed away the memory. "I've been talking at you nonstop for almost three hours. Would have thought you'd be glad for the silence."

"So long as there's nothing bothering you. Things got a little painful there towards the end. Talking about your cousin."

Her concern touched him. It had been a long while since someone had worried about his state of mind. Just for that, Whit gave her a smile. "I'm fine," he assured her. "Monty's death hurt like hell, I'm not going to lie, but it's been more than eleven years. I'm over it now."

"You never talked about him when we were in college."

"Never saw a reason to," he replied. "Why depress people by bringing up my dead cousin?" Far easier to keep the grief to himself.

"You must miss him."

"I do, but like I said…"

"It was years ago. This place is nice."

Smart woman, she got the hint.

"Definitely hip and trendy," he said, handing her a menu. "I thought you'd been here?"

"Only read about it. If I'm at the library, it's because I'm working. You're not the only one who doesn't want to sit in a library bar alone."

"Fair point," Whit said. He skimmed the menu for nonalcoholic options. "Although I'm surprised none of your dates ever suggested the place." This was exactly the kind of place he would take her. Literary-inspired cocktails at a library? Couldn't get more Jamie-like.

"I'd need to have a date first."

Wait, she meant recently, right? Whit looked up to see Jamie, across the table, trying to hide her blush behind the eight-by-ten menu. "Sounded a lot less pathetic in my head," she said. "What I meant to say was that dating has taken a back seat to work these last few months."

"Join the club. Recovery isn't the best time to get involved with someone." That was one reason, anyway.

"But," he said, brightening, "we're here now, so we might as well enjoy ourselves. Pick your poison, as they say. You are allowed to drink alcohol around me," he added when he spied her biting her lip.

"Are you sure?"

"Positive," he told her. "I don't expect everyone in the world to conform to my sobriety. Besides, some of these drinks look...interesting. Which one strikes your fancy?"

"Hard choice," she said as she skimmed the

paper menu. "How does one choose between Dorian Gray and War and Peace?" Together, they chuckled over the literary drink names while waiting for the waitress. Whit sat back and listened as Jamie added an interpretation of each drink based on its literary namesake. The War and Peace lasted forever. The bartender was watching if you ordered the 1984. She told him she would order the Dorian Gray on the off chance it would keep her forever youthful, not that Whit thought it mattered. After hours of listening to himself talk, her voice sounded like a cheery melody. It cleared his head and smoothed out the tension in his shoulders.

"What do you do these days?" he asked, once the server had come and gone.

She was playing with the edge of the menu but stopped when he spoke. "What do you mean?"

"I know you said dating had taken a back seat to work, but you can't be working all the time. You must have some fun. What do you do?"

"Nothing exciting, I'm afraid. Work out, go shopping with Kish. Every once in a while, she drags me out for drinks with her friends from the lab or guys from Terrance's law firm. To be honest, I spend most of my time working. I don't do a lot of playing around."

"Never?"

"Not if I want to pay off my loans and put some

money in the bank. You've never been poor, Whit. It's not fun."

Thinking of his own crash, Whit nodded in agreement. "Lots of things in life aren't fun."

"It's funny," Jamie said, her finger drawing lazy circles on the table surface. "When you're younger and fantasizing about the future, you think life is going to be all sunshine and romantic adventures. Then you grow up and realize they're called fantasies for a reason."

"Wow, when did you get so cynical?" he asked.

Something unreadable flickered across her face. "I prefer the term *realistic*."

Didn't matter which term she used, her answer bothered him. This was the second time she'd made such a comment; she said something similar when they'd had lunch together last week. He didn't like hearing her sound so disenchanted. Where had his Jamie—that is, the Jamie he knew in college, the one who was dreamy and idealistic—gone?

"Now it's my turn to ask another question," Jamie said just as the server arrived with their drinks and a cheese platter.

"No fair," Whit replied as he reached for a slice of gouda. "You've been asking questions all day. Only fair I get to ask you more than one."

"Technically you've already asked three, but all right. What would like to know?"

Good question. Since he'd already shelved the question he really wanted to ask, Whit had to think. He felt a little like the boy granted three wishes, wanting to make his questions really count. Thing was, he knew a lot about Jamie already.

Or did he? His picture of her high school years was certainly way off.

In the end, he decided to take a page from her book. "What is your earliest childhood memory?"

She paused mid-sip. "Seriously?"

"Why not?" he replied with a shrug. "Your talk about high school has made me curious. I want to know about Jamie Rutkowski, the early years. What is your earliest memory?"

While she thought, he watched her index finger run up and down the stem of her glass. Maybe he should have asked if her hands ever stilled.

"My stuffed pig," she told him. "My dad gave me this stuffed pig that played music. I carried him everywhere. I remember he used to sit on my lap when my mom read me bedtime stories."

"I bet you were freaking adorable," Whit said. A little brown-haired toddler carting a stuffed farm animal around.

"My mom said I was, but I'm not sure she was objective. All mothers think their babies are adorable."

So long as they don't get dirt on their Prada jacket, Whit thought.

"What happened to the pig? He still around? Hidden in a nightstand drawer?"

"I wish. One of the kids from my mom's day care got a hold of him and decided he needed a bath. Dunked him in the toilet. Piggy wasn't so nice to have around after that."

"I bet. Sorry."

She waved it off. "Hazard of having a day care in your house."

Whit tried to imagine a house filled with other people's children. "Must have been chaotic," he said, thinking of his own house. It too had a lot of people coming and going. Artists, musicians, gurus. Whoever suited his parents' fancy at the time.

"It had its moments. But when I was little I had people to play with, and then when I got older, I could count on them going home so I could have dinner alone with my parents, so it wasn't all bad. And when things got too loud for me in the house, I had the library to go to."

"Were you lonely?" It was the question she'd asked of him.

If Jamie was annoyed about his turning the tables on her, you couldn't tell from her face. She took a sip from her drink and set it on the table with certainty. "I was too busy to think about it."

A person's loneliness was no reason to smile, but Whit found himself smiling anyway. Maybe because she'd used almost his exact same words. He felt understood. The knowledge caused a comforting fullness in his chest. Too comforting, really. He wasn't sure he knew how to deal with it, so he backed away.

Instead, he pointed to Jamie's half-finished drink. "How's the cocktail?"

"Delicious," Jamie replied.

She forced herself to smile so he wouldn't see her spirit flagging at the abrupt change of topic. When Whit asked her about loneliness, she'd paraphrased his words on impulse, wanting him to know he wasn't the only one who'd grown up surrounded by people, and yet alone. The message was received. There was no mistaking the gratitude in his smile, and for a second, the embers of the connection they'd once shared flickered with life, only to flame out just as quickly. Whit wasn't interested in reconnecting with her romantically. She reminded herself she didn't care, but that didn't stop the old feelings of inadequacy from making an appearance.

"I never would have thought of a cocktail made of gin and herbal tea, but damn if it doesn't work," she told him.

"I'll take your word for it," Whit replied. "Feels

a little weird, being able to order a drink in the public library. I feel like I should whisper."

Jamie felt her smile muscles relax. "I know what you mean." As it was, neither of them was speaking very loudly.

"At least the place doesn't smell musty. You ever notice how some buildings, even if they've been renovated, have an atmosphere about them? Like the air has a weight to it? I'm not sure what you would call it. *Musty* isn't the right word."

"Technically, it is, but I know what you mean. The atmosphere has a kind of gravitas," Jamie replied. "Like it's reminding visitors they've entered some place important. You can feel the importance of what's inside."

"Exactly. I never appreciated it until recently. The concept, not the smell."

"I like the smell," she said. "Sounds weird, I know, but it's like smelling a part of the past." She thought back to the old buildings on campus and her library back home. "I've always been a sucker for historical buildings."

"You'd have a field day in Europe then. There are towns where you can't throw a rock without hitting a historic building, or at least one that has seen history."

"Sounds lovely," she said. "When I was in high school, I thought it would be awesome to visit England and see all the castles and walk where people like King Arthur walked. I know," she held up a hand before he could say anything, "the whole Lady of the Lake thing is a myth."

She watched Whit's finger tracing the outline of his teacup. His eyes were lowered, his lashes a thick, sandy veil blocking his expression. "That sounds…"

"Silly?" she supplied. She agreed. If she went to England now, she would tackle a more organized itinerary rather than waste her time off crisscrossing the country tracing a made-up legend.

"I was going to say 'interesting.' Definitely a different experience than the one I had."

Knowing how his experience had ended, Jamie hadn't planned on talking about Europe until their next meeting. There were a ton of questions she wanted to ask, but this wasn't the time. Especially not now, with people sitting at the nearby tables. Better she stayed quiet and let Whit dictate the conversation. "My original plan was to play polo for just a summer and then backpack around the continent," he said.

"Alone?"

"Why not? There are always other backpackers you can join up with. Plus, I figured I could use the time to contemplate what I wanted to do when I returned to the States in the spring."

Only he didn't return. He stayed several more

years. "What happened to change your plans?" she asked.

"I ended up joining some teammates and traveling to the Riviera. Hard to be alone with your thoughts when you've got three buddies hauling you to a nightclub every night."

Staying too busy to notice. Jamie broke a little at the thought. How had she not noticed Whit's loneliness while they were together?

He had gone back to tracing his cup. Round and round as though following an endless path. "Makes you wonder what would have happened if I carried through with my original plan, doesn't it?" he said in a weary voice. "Might have saved myself a lot of trouble. Guess we'll never know."

Jamie didn't know how to respond to that. She didn't like hearing him sound so defeated. "'To regret deeply, is to start afresh,'" she murmured.

"What?"

Under other circumstances, she'd think his confused expression would be adorable. "It's a Thoreau quote. I got it in a fortune cookie once. I took it to mean that if you're truly sorry about something, you can change and start again."

"What if being sorry isn't enough?"

She answered honestly. "I don't know."

"Me neither," he replied.

With that, the shadow that lurked behind his eyes reared up to wrap him in despair. Something haunted him, thought Jamie. Something beyond his addiction. What was it? The answer was, she suspected, the driving force behind this memoir.

This wasn't the time or place to push, though. After dozens of these interviews, she knew that a subject only revealed what they were ready to reveal. Eventually, Whit would drop his guard enough to share. Until then, she could only think of one way to respond.

Reaching across the table, she took his hand. "From where I sit, you've started plenty afresh."

Even with his head lowered, she could see his small smile. "Good Lord, that's corny," he said. "Thank you."

Before she could pull her hand away, he pressed it to his lips.

CHAPTER FOUR

JAMIE'S BREATH CAUGHT. He might as well have kissed her full on the mouth, the way her skin reacted. It was as though someone had carbonated her nerve endings with tiny bubbles that moved from her hand right up her arm.

"I... I need to go," she stammered. "Keisha is expecting me."

"Right, the dress fitting." Whit released her hand. The bubbles remained. It took everything she had not to immediately start rubbing her skin. Instead, she stood up and reached for her coat, which hung on the back of her seat.

"Here, let me." Whit was on her side of the table before she could say anything, holding her coat. "Childhood etiquette lessons, remember?"

Jamie did. They'd joked about it at college, how he automatically reverted to gentleman status whenever there was a door to be opened.

"Thank you," she replied, pretending not to feel his breath on her neck as she slipped into her sleeves.

She really needed to get a hold of herself. It was a kiss of gratitude, for crying out loud. There was zero need to get this worked up about it. Looking at her drink, she saw there were still a few sips left. "I'm sorry to bolt out of here so quickly, but the last thing I want to do is keep the bride waiting."

"Completely understandable. No sense waking the bridezilla. I should get to the airport anyway. Do you need a ride? I can have my car drop you off."

Had he had a driver waiting for him all this time? "Thank you, but no," she told him. "The boutique is right on Newberry Street. I can walk."

"Are you sure?"

"Yes. The fresh air will help me clear my head."

He chuckled. "Drink was that potent?"

"Something like that." Maybe it was the drink making her overreact. "I'll email my outline to you sometime in the next few days and we can talk about doing another set of interviews."

"Sounds good."

There was an awkward silence as the two of them stood there, looking at each other. Jamie knew she should say goodbye, but her feet didn't want to move. If she didn't know better, she'd say they were acting like it was the end of a date, expectant and uncertain as to what they should do next.

"Screw it," Whit said suddenly and, reaching out, he pulled her into a hug. Traces of bay rum aftershave clung to his shirt, carrying with its spicy aroma the memory of their bodies wrapped together in a dorm room bed. It was a bad idea, but Jamie inhaled and let the image wash over her anyway.

The moment was over in a blink. She'd barely filled her lungs when Whit released her.

"See you soon," he said.

Giving a nod, she turned and hurried toward the exit. Her head was spinning. Definitely the alcohol, she decided. Otherwise, she might be in real trouble here.

"I knew that shade of green would look good on you," Keisha said. Sitting on a stool in the corner of Dona Tessia's bridal salon, she watched while a seamstress pinned the hem of Jamie's dress. "Put your hair up and get you some blingy earrings and you'll look amazing."

Maybe, thought Jamie. Despite her threats to the contrary, Keisha had selected a gorgeous bridesmaid gown for her. Forest green, the gown had a plunging halter neck and a full pleated skirt. Jamie wasn't feeling the amazingness, though. She'd rushed nearly three blocks before her head finally stopped spinning. And another two before she stopped thinking about how good it felt to have his arms around her again.

That's what happened when you drank with nothing more a cheese plate in her stomach. Next meeting, no alcohol. No going out after the session period.

Unless Whit looked as lost as he had today.

"You okay?" In the mirror, Keisha's reflection was studying her with concern. "You're not oohing and ahhing over the dress like I thought you would."

"I'm too focused on not falling off this tiny platform," she replied. The small circle stood a foot off the floor, and the sample pair of shoes she'd borrowed were a size too big. "If I move, I'll screw up the hem."

Her friend didn't look convinced, but for once, didn't argue. She crossed and uncrossed her legs, offering a flash of purple stiletto before resting her chin in the palm of her hand. "How'd your client meeting go?" she asked. "Productive?"

"Subtle, Kish. You know perfectly well I met with Whit today. And yes, it was a productive meeting."

"Good to hear. You got a lot of good information to write about, then."

"Yes, I did." Although she wasn't sure she'd call discovering Whit had a lonely childhood and then lost his cousin and best friend at seventeen *good*. "It's going to be a powerful story."

"I'll have to take your word for it," Keisha said, "since you won't tell us what the book's about."

There was no mistaking the hurt in her friend's

voice. Keisha never did take well to being kept in the dark.

"Give me a break, Kish. This isn't my story to talk about. It's Whit's."

"Never stopped you before."

"Yeah, well, we've never both known the client before. Telling you would feel too much like talking behind his back." Down by her feet, the seamstress motioned for Jamie to rotate left, saving her from having to see Keisha's annoyed reflection. "When Whit's ready to share, I'm sure he will."

"I can tell you one thing," she added, as an appeasement. "I'm realizing that I read him completely wrong back in college."

"What does that mean?"

It meant he wasn't the goldenly perfect man she'd thought him to be. The popularity, the smiles, the fun-loving living for the moment masked a whole lot of pain. The boy she'd dated, Jamie was starting to think, didn't really exist.

"Only that there was a lot about him I didn't know," she told Keisha. "There was a lot more depth to him than I ever realized. He's really quite…" She searched for the right word. "Vulnerable."

"Huh."

Jamie looked over her shoulder. "What?"

"Nothing," her friend said. "Except every time you talk about him, you're selling me on some newly discovered facet of his personality. He's different, he's vulnerable."

"I didn't realize describing someone was a problem."

"It isn't, except when the description sounds like someone's relighting her torch."

"Will you shut up. Saying a few nice things about a person doesn't mean I have feelings for them. I've said nice things about a lot of people."

"You weren't madly in love with those people."

"I'm not madly in love with Whit either," Jamie replied quickly. Anymore.

The seamstress indicated she was finished, allowing her to step down off the pedestal. Once on level ground, she walked over and stood in front of Keisha. "When you ghostwrite a person's story, you end up getting to know them inside and out. It's only logical that I'd learn new things about Whit too, and some of them will be positive. That doesn't mean squat."

"I suppose," Keisha replied, looking down at her jeans. "I just remember how…"

Jamie didn't need the reminder. "Trust me, Kish, I'm not stupid enough to fall for him a second time."

"Excuse me, miss?" It was the seamstress interrupting them. "I think your phone is ringing."

Sure enough, familiar music was coming from her bag. Taking care not to step on the newly pinned hem, Jamie shuffled her way to a nearby chair where she'd deposited her belongings earlier.

To her embarrassment, her pulse quickened when she saw the number.

"Hey," Whit said when she answered. His voice was soft in her ear.

She closed her eyes to avoid remembering the feeling of his arms around her, but the memory proved too strong.

"I wanted to find out if you made your meeting with Keisha on time, or if she released the kraken on you."

Jamie's face broke out in a smile. Feeling her cheeks growing warm, she turned her head to keep Keisha from seeing. "Wrong creature, and yes, I was right on time."

"Good. I was afraid I delayed you by chatting too long."

"You're supposed to chat," she told him. "That's the whole point."

"I meant after," he said, sounding like he was sharing a secret. "Thank you for indulging me."

"You don't have to thank me," she said.

It was the perfect time to tell him that this afternoon was a one-off, but the words didn't want to form. With Keisha staring at the back of her head, it was hard to talk freely. She didn't want to run the risk of her friend misunderstanding and blowing things out of proportion. "I enjoyed talking with you," she added.

Hearing the silence that greeted her comment, she was afraid she'd gone too far, but a moment later, Whit was back. "When I landed in LaGuardia, I realized there was a question I forgot to ask you."

"What's that?" Hopefully it wasn't anything super personal.

"Do you have a cat?"

What? The question didn't make sense. Why would he ask that?

"I was thinking about that stray cat that used to poke around your dormitory. The one you named."

"You mean O'Malley?" Jamie hadn't thought about the big yellow tiger cat in years. She used to feed it scraps from the dining hall. "What about him?"

"You told me that when you graduated and got your own place, you were going to get a cat that looked just like him. I was wondering if you ever did?"

He remembered the stray cat? How many times had she talked with Keisha about meeting a man who paid attention to the little details? The idea that Whit had been paying that kind of attention to her back then…

Or maybe he simply had a really good memory, she warned herself, telling the flutter in her stomach to calm down.

"Afraid not," she told him. "Keisha was allergic and then when she moved out, I was too busy with work to visit the shelter."

"Pity, but life happens, right?" His voice brightened. "On the plus side, now I know what to get you for Christmas. I'd have to get you a pair, though, so they can keep each other company."

Jamie laughed. "Why stop at two? Go for three and make me the crazy cat lady."

"Don't be silly. Everyone knows that takes four cats."

"Now you're just being silly." Keisha cleared her throat, putting an end to the conversation. "I need to go," Jamie told him hurriedly. "I'm still in the gown. I'm glad you got back to New York all right."

They repeated their plans to touch base once she sent him over her outline and said goodbye. Jamie continued holding the phone for a minute after Whit hung up. Without his voice in her ear, the salon seemed overly quiet.

Finally, she slipped the phone back into her bag and turned around, only to find Keisha standing two feet away. Her friend folded her arms across her chest and arched her perfectly groomed brow. "Not stupid enough to fall for him a second time, huh?" she asked.

"Oh, for crying out loud. It was just a silly conversation." Brushing past her friend, she headed to the fitting room to change back into her street clothes. Honestly, like she told Whit, the woman saw romance in everything. She was not falling for the man again.

After all, if he didn't fall in love with her the first time around, he sure as hell wasn't going to now.

Jamie didn't hear from Whit until Tuesday the following week, in part because she dragged her feet on the outline. Normally she prided herself on her fast turnarounds. Every time she sat down to work, however, she found herself remembering Keisha's skeptical expression. As a result, she developed a minor case of procrastinationitis. Her bestie was wrong. Sure, she felt compassion for Whit, she appreciated this more open, thoughtful side of him, and she was recognizing her own misguided beliefs about him, but that was as far as her emotions went. If she slipped up occasionally, and physically reacted to his touch, or his scent, or his smile, or his voice or his…anything, it was merely a result of triggered memories.

After four days of arguing these points in her head, she finally drafted something and hit Send. Twenty-four hours later, her phone rang. In the middle of an incredibly vivid dream about singing stray cats who smelled of bay rum, she first thought the music was part of the act. Slowly she realized the source of the sound and snatched the phone off her nightstand.

"Hello?" she grumbled, her voice heavy with sleep.

"Hello, sleepyhead. Did I wake you?"

With her eyes closed, Whit's voice sounded like it was coming from beside her instead of the phone. Jamie instinctively answered with a lazy, "Mmm…?"

"Must be nice. It's after nine."

What? Jamie sat up in her empty bed. Checking the phone, she saw he was right. "I must have forgotten to set my alarm."

"Tsk, tsk, tsk," he chided. "Everyone blames the alarm. I'm disappointed, Rutkowski. I thought you'd be more creative."

"Sorry. Brilliance comes with revision." Stretching her arm over her head, she yawned, then settled back against her headboard and forced her sleepy brain into business mode. "What can I do for you?"

"I read your proposed outline. It looks good. I'm assuming you'll add more detail as we go along."

"Precisely. Like I said…"

"Brilliance comes with revision."

Even though he couldn't see her face, Jamie

smirked. "In this case it comes with more information." Such as whatever had happened in Europe that drove him to writing this book. "We still have a lot of ground to cover."

The silence on the other end felt heavy with reluctance. "We don't have to continue if you don't want to," she reminded him. "It's your story; if you want to scrap the book, it's your call."

His response was quick if not emphatic. "No, I want to do this. I need to do this. What's the next step?"

"Depends on how fast you'd like to work. Usually at this point I spend a few days, maybe a week, with the client and we go over the entire story in depth from beginning to end. Then I go home to write the first draft. If that doesn't work for you, we can continue meeting once a week for a month or so. Again, your story, your call."

She heard him take a deep breath. "All at once would be better. I'd rather not stretch things out. Do you think you could start tomorrow?"

Jamie sat up a little straighter. He wasn't kidding about wanting to get the process over with. Quickly checking her calendar app, she saw that, other than a few reschedulable tasks, she was free until early the next week. "Um, sure. I'll have to call around to some of the work share spaces to see if there's a meeting room free. I'm not sure if the library conference room will be open on such short notice, though." If desperate, they could maybe find a place at the Mandarin. Or use her apartment. She thought of Whit's overwhelming presence filling her living room, his long arms stretched across the back of her sofa in that gracefully confident way he had about him.

Maybe not her apartment.

"Actually…" Whit's voice pulled her back to the call. "I was wondering if we could do the interview here."

"You mean in Manhattan?"

"No, Iceland. Yes, Manhattan. I, um… I'd feel more comfortable talking on home turf, instead some random share space."

When he put it that way… Jamie chewed the inside of her cheek. Interviews did always go better when the subject was at ease, and it wouldn't be the first time she'd traveled to another location. There was no reason to hesitate. Or for her pulse to race.

"Jamie?"

"Sure," she replied. "I don't mind traveling in."

"Great. I'll have my assistant make the arrangements and email you with the details."

They spent a few more minutes discussing particulars. "I won't say I'm looking forward to baring my soul," Whit said when they'd finished, "but I am looking forward to seeing you again."

Thank goodness this was a phone conversation,

because she smiled way wider than was merited. "Same here," she told him. After saying good-bye, she tossed the phone on the bed beside her. Looked like she would be spending her day packing for New York.

Now if she could just get her stomach to stop bouncing like a teenage girl's, everything would be fine.

Whit placed the handset back on the cradle. Jamie was coming to Manhattan. By this time next week, she would know all about Europe and the yacht party in Capri.

She'd never look at him the same way again.

So what? he asked himself as he ran a hand across his jaw. The whole point of the book was to let the entire world know what he did. Why was he so fixated on the opinion of one ex-girlfriend?

Because Jamie was the only ex-girlfriend whose memory stuck with him, that's why. The only one he wished he hadn't left behind. And who still looked at him with compassion.

He thought back to those last few minutes in the Map Room, when she'd reached for his hand. Nothing since returning from Europe had grounded him like her brief touch. He felt connected, so much so he'd had to try for more by hugging her goodbye. Her hair smelled like lavender, he thought with a smile.

He wanted more of the feeling. More grounding. How long, he wondered, could he delay the inevitable letdown? One day more? Two? Eventually he would have no choice but to tell her that he'd caused a woman's death. How much compassion would he see in her eyes then? For that matter, would she even be able to look him in the face?

"You're only as sick as your secrets," they'd told him in rehab. "The only way to truly heal is to expose everything to the light and face the consequences." Whit had been avoiding the consequences for two years, thinking that if he gave enough of himself, did enough good deeds, it wouldn't matter if his crimes stayed secret forever. He'd been wrong. His burden weighed as heavily on him today as it did on day one. Talking to Jamie about that baseball player had made him realize that if he truly wanted closure, he had to let the secret out. Sharing in front of a recovery group wouldn't be enough; he needed to tell the whole sordid family story in print.

He was going to disappoint a lot of people. Family. Friends. Didn't matter. He deserved whatever backlash he received. Including losing Jamie's compassion.

In the meantime, at least he could do right by Jamie and make her trip to New York as comfortable as possible. He buzzed for his assistant.

CHAPTER FIVE

FOR THE REST of the morning through lunch, Whit distracted himself by reading grant recommendations. By early afternoon his back and shoulders had had enough. He was in the process of stretching out his spine when a knock sounded on his office door.

"Excuse me, Mr. Martin." His assistant appeared in the doorway. "Ms. Rutkowski is here. She's waiting in the lobby."

"Thank you." Suddenly the tightness between his shoulder blades eased. Grabbing his suit jacket from the back of his chair, he strode toward the lobby, only to draw up short when he reached the entrance.

Jamie sat against the wall, scrolling through her phone. Amid the black-and-gray furnishings, she was a ray of sunshine, bright and pretty. Funny thing was, she was wearing the same black-and-white dress that she'd worn to lunch the day after the engagement party, but somehow the lack of color looked vibrant on her. Had she always lit up a room like this? The engagement party didn't count because she'd been dressed to kill. He didn't remember being this awestruck before.

She looked up and it was like someone turned on a light.

"You made it." He moved forward, planning to greet her with a hug, only to be blocked by a notebook she clutched to her chest at the last minute. He settled for awkwardly clasping her elbow. "How was the flight?"

"Eye-opening. I've never flown in a private helicopter before. Felt like I was the President."

"Too bad they don't allow rooftop landings. You could have felt really special," Whit said. No sooner did he say it than the phrase "not that you aren't special already" popped into his head.

"Good thing they don't. My head might have exploded. The drivers and the flight were enough."

"We definitely wouldn't want your head to explode, would we? Come on, I'll show you around the place. Give you the grand tour before we begin."

"You know…" she said as they started walking, "you didn't have to go to so much trouble. Usually my clients have me book a flight and put in for reimbursement."

"I know," he replied. Only he wanted to go to the trouble. He wanted her to enjoy the special treatment. "What good is having a helicopter if you can't treat your friends to easy commutes?"

He guided her down the corridor. "Do you travel for work often?"

"Depends on how many books I have scheduled. At least four or five times a year," she replied. "I prefer to meet with my subjects face-to-face. It helps me capture their personality on the page."

"Wait, does that mean you're writing four or five books a year?" In his head, he roughly estimated how much writing that would be. "Doesn't sound like it leaves much time for doing anything else."

"I told you I was too busy working to have a social life," she replied. "Now, show me this foundation of yours."

If she was hoping to change the topic, she'd said the magic words. If there was one thing Whit enjoyed, it was showing off his foundation. The work they did made him proud. As they walked past the glass block walls and modular offices, he explained some of the programs they were hoping to establish. Every so often Jamie would ask a question, but mostly she let him talk, the expression on her face one of true interest. He figured she was probably paying such close attention because the information made good fodder for the book, but that didn't stop Whit from feeling pleased.

On the wall inside the conference center hung poster-size news articles about the Martin family and their philanthropic efforts. A concession to his grandfather when establishing the foundation, who'd wanted the family tradition prominently displayed.

For some reason, as Whit watched her reading them, the memory of her studying popped into his head. She was always reading and writing in school. Propped against the dorm wall, legs curled under her, her mouth parted a little in concentration. Her eyes would get this dreamy, faraway look. Losing herself in the story, she'd said when Whit had remarked on it once.

That was the day she'd told him she planned to become a writer. Practically talked his ear off about the idea she had for a novel.

Whit had never said, but he'd always admired her for it. She wasn't afraid to dream. There had been a kind of innocence to how she'd approached the world. In her mind, all she'd had to do was want something badly enough and it would happen. The law of attraction, Jamie style, he'd called it.

He stole another look at profile. Why, then, had she shelved all her dreams in favor of ghostwriting other people's stories? To pay her bills, she'd said when they were at the Map Room. A perfectly logical reason, but he couldn't shake the notion that there was more to the story than that. After all, couldn't she do both? Write for herself and for others?

* * *

"This is amazing," Jamie said. "I had no idea your organization funded all of this. You must be very proud."

"We all are. The foundation is a group effort." He looked at the center poster, which featured a photo of his grandfather and great uncles at the initial foundation announcement. "It's funny. If you had told me in college that I would spend my days giving away the family money, I'd have laughed in your face."

"Didn't your family want you to go into politics?"

"One of the chosen Martin paths." He'd forgotten he'd told her about it. "Rehab pretty much put a nail in that coffin." That and the fact he'd rather cut off his ears.

"From the looks of things, you landed in precisely the right spot. I imagine those guys in the photo are as impressed as I am."

Her words warmed him from the inside out. *God, I want to kiss you right now*, he thought. Too bad it would probably earn him a slap across the face.

He settled for a sincere, "Thank you. That means a lot."

There was nothing he'd like to do more than bask in her approval all afternoon long. Unfortunately, he knew that wasn't possible. Eventually

they were going to have to start work on the book
and he was going to have to talk about Europe.

He wasn't looking forward to it.

"Personally, I would have called myself an advanced amateur. I became a professional by accident."

Jamie was sitting at the conference table in
Whit's office, listening to him explain the sport
of polo. Most of the information she already knew
from her research, but she figured discussing the
sport might make for an easier transition into the
more difficult topics.

Plus, it gave her a chance to acclimate to her
surroundings.

His office was like him. Sleek and impressive. On one end, light filtered through a wall of
glass blocks. On the other, a window looked out
onto West Broadway. She could see the Freedom
Tower in the distance.

Hard to believe that less than four hours ago,
she was stuffing clothes into a suitcase. Two lim-
ousines and a private helicopter later, here she
was in a Martin-owned Manhattan skyscraper
while her driver took care of checking her into
her hotel. It was all so surreal. She felt spoiled
and special. Meanwhile, for Whit, it was an ev-
eryday occurrence.

Whit. He was back in corporate mode in a dark

suit and red tie. Actually, he was in shirtsleeves at the moment, his suit jacket slung over the back of his chair. Even so, he and the office fit like hand and glove. Sitting at his desk, he looked like royalty seated on a throne. It was an overwhelmingly attractive look on him.

"And how does one 'accidentally' turn professional?" she asked him. Most professional sports she knew about involved years of training.

"It's easier than you think. The summer before graduation, I played a match against a visiting British team. I got to know the coaches, and they invited me to join them when I finished school."

"They must have been pretty impressed."

"I held my own. Plus, I could afford to buy my own string of polo ponies. Always an added benefit."

"So, you moved to Europe and became a professional player." He was right, it did sound easy.

"Actually, I started as an advanced amateur. One of the beauties of polo is that amateurs and professionals often play together. Anyway, a couple months in, a player broke his leg during a Cup Tournament and the coach asked if I would fill in for the game. I played well enough that they asked if I would travel with them. And just like that, I was playing professionally."

Jamie shook her head. "Unbelievable."

"The first couple years, it was a dream come

true. Even my grandfather couldn't give me too much of a hard time because being a professional meant I had an actual career. Not an easy one either. Wasn't like we sat around working on our tans until tournament day. During the season we trained and practiced like any other professional athlete."

"Not all the time," she noted dryly. "I saw the photos."

Whit flashed what was becoming a trademark grin. "I never said we didn't have fun."

He began telling her about life on the circuit, painting a picture of excitement and comradery that would be romantic if not for the bittersweet look in his eyes. He spoke about his teammates and horses the way one talked about a lost summer where everything was tainted with a sheen of regret.

"Sounds like a fun way to make a living, especially if you enjoyed what you were doing."

"I did. I liked playing polo and being on a team. They were good guys."

"What did you do in the offseason?"

"Didn't really have one," Whit said. "You can pretty much play year-round if you're willing to travel."

Keeping him busy. She was seeing a pattern here. "I pretty much played nonstop until the Gold Cup tournament in Sotogrande."

As soon as he said the words, a blind came down over his features. Jamie could feel the energy changing in the room.

"What happened?"

"Got too close to another player and our horses collided. I was thrown off."

"Oh, my God." Her hand clapped over her mouth. That was what? A six-foot drop? While moving at speed? He could have been killed. "How badly were you hurt?"

"I broke a few ribs, dislocated my shoulder, had a mild concussion." He rattled off injuries like it was a grocery list. "Wrecked the hell out of my back too, though that was mostly soft tissue. At the hospital they told me I was lucky."

"You were. If you had landed on your neck or skull…" She shuddered to think what might have happened. The idea of a world without Whit in it made her sick to her stomach. "Thank goodness you survived."

"I survived all right." The black enamel of the pen caught the light as he tossed it onto the desk. "Twenty-four hours later and I was back in my hotel with a bottle of painkillers."

Oh. They'd reached the beginning of the end. She forced herself not to respond aloud. Sometimes the best interview tactic was silence. People, as a rule, didn't like dead air, and instinctively sought to fill it with conversation. In this case, the silence was thick and heavy. She could see the struggle playing out on Whit's face as he thought about where and how to begin. "I couldn't do much," he finally said. "It hurt to move, hurt to breathe. The painkillers were the only thing that made it bearable. I burned through the prescription in a little over a week and had to bum some off my teammates."

Jamie could already guess the rest of the story. "And you couldn't stop." The words hung between them.

Instead of answering, however, he removed his glasses and began to clean the lenses with a silk square he'd taken out of his desk drawer. His expression was blank. "You know the thing about soft tissue injuries?" he asked. "They can take forever to heal, especially if you are riding a horse for hours every day."

Meaning the pain continued. Meaning the pills continued. But then, if he was dependent on them, the pills would have also made him feel like he was in pain every time they wore off. A twisted chicken-or-the-egg scenario.

"I'm sorry," she whispered only for Whit to shrug her off.

"For what? You didn't make me take the pills. I swallowed them all by myself without any help."

Maybe, but that didn't make her feel any less compassion for him. His was a sad and common story. "You're not the first athlete to wind up in a downward drug spiral," she told him. "What happened to you can happen to anyone. There's no need to continue to punish yourself."

"Ha!" His bark of laughter gave her a chill. "You might think differently once you hear the rest of the story. Things got way worse before they got better."

"How so?"

Jamie waited while he fiddled with the pen he'd retrieved. Twisting the top back and forth. She was rubbing the side of her pen smooth herself.

Outside, the sky was not quite dark. The days of pitch-black commutes were past. Still, it was gray enough that the buildings glowed.

"I could use some air," Whit said abruptly. "How about you?"

In other words, he wasn't ready to answer her question and so was shutting down for the night. Frustrated as she was about him pausing right as they were getting into the thick of his story, Jamie understood. For all his desire to share, Whit wasn't used to talking out loud about his addiction. The little he'd already shared had taken a toll on him. If what he was going to share tomorrow was so much worse, she could understand why he needed to regroup tonight.

"Now that you say it, fresh air sounds good," she said.

Having received his reprieve, Whit's body relaxed. "I know the perfect place," he said. "Follow me."

You're a coward, Martin.

Whit ignored his inner critic, even though the noisy bastard was right. It was his story, and if he wanted to drag his feet in telling it, then that was his prerogative. Whoever said confession was good for the soul was a liar. He felt terrible.

Because you haven't really confessed anything yet, and you know it.

Whatever. The secret would be out soon enough. Then he'd see if his soul felt better. Right now, he'd enjoy Jamie's compassion while he had it.

Most of the office staff knocked off around four o'clock, meaning the building was nearly empty when they stepped out of his office. Usually he preferred when the place was bustling, but tonight he was grateful for the solitude.

The two of them stood in the office's empty reception area and buttoned their coats. "Where are we walking to?" Jamie asked. "Are we going someplace specific, or walking back around the block?"

"Neither." He pushed the Up button. "This time of day the sidewalk is too crowded and noisy. The building has a rooftop terrace. Up there we can hear ourselves think."

The building's rooftop terrace wasn't as fancy as some of the others in the city. Basically, it was a large teak square with containers of flowering plants at each corner. But it was peaceful and had a beautiful view. To Whit it was a little slice of heaven.

"In warm weather, we set out furniture and umbrellas," Whit said as he unlocked the access door with his key.

This time of year, the furniture was put away, and vinyl covers placed on the stoneware containers, leaving nothing but open space and a handful of spotlights to light visitors' way.

"Nice isn't it? People come up here for lunch or meetings so they can get some fresh air without battling the crowds." He held open the door to let Jamie through first.

"Lately, I've been coming here after everyone's gone home. No one comes up in the off-season, meaning I have the place to myself. Look over there and you'll see the Empire State Building. That's the Chrysler Building a little further down."

"Wow," Jamie said as she walked to the square's center. "When you first suggested the roof, I pictured tar paper and air vents. The last thing I expected was a terrace."

"New York's not like Boston. Here we make green spaces wherever we can."

"I can see why people enjoy it up here. It's a lot quieter than on the street. A little breezier than I expected, though," she added as she turned up the collar on her coat.

"Sorry. I should have warned you."

Out of habit, he'd put on his scarf at the same time as his coat. "Hold on," he said. He draped the red cashmere over her head like a shawl. "Tie this around your head. At least your ears will be warm."

"Don't mind if I do," she replied.

While Jamie fussed with the scarf, Whit wandered to the edge of the platform. Even nineteen stories up, the lights from Manhattan illuminated the sky. The skyscraper across the street looked like an uneven chess board as office lights began turning off one by one. "Something about being up here makes the rest of the world feel very far away."

"It should. We're nineteen floors up."

"Thank you for stating the obvious." His sarcasm might have sounded sharper if he wasn't smiling when he spoke. Below the people and cars crawled along.

"Plenty of people tonight," Jamie said. "Look at them all."

"Every once in a while, when I come up here, I try to count exactly how many people there are in this one block."

"Sounds like a challenge."

Whit turned toward her. "What can I say? I like a…challenge." The final word stuck in his throat. With the scarf tied like that, only Jamie's face was visible, the lights giving her skin a Madonna-like glow. She looked… Whit didn't know the word. He'd always thought her beautiful, but tonight's beauty had a different quality to it. Something more. He couldn't find the words, but he felt it. A warm tightness filled his chest. "Better?" he asked.

"My ears definitely are. Not sure how long my legs will last."

He looked down at the hem of her coat, where several inches of her legs were exposed. There was only a thin layer of nylon stocking protecting her skin.

"We can go back inside if you want," he said.

"I'll be all right if I keep moving," she said. "The cold air feels good. Are you feeling better?"

"I wasn't feeling bad."

She lifted her brows.

"All right, maybe a little bad," he conceded. "I…talking about those days after the accident… It's shameful remembering how weak I was." Feeling the heat rising to his cheeks, he looked away.

Staring at his feet couldn't stop Jamie's scrutiny or his awareness of it. "You know addiction's a disease, right? That it has nothing to do with weakness?" she asked.

A lecture they'd hammered home endlessly at the clinic. "Thing is, logically, I understand what the experts are saying, but when I think of how easily I fell into it..." He still remembered the pain and loneliness of those days and how good oblivion had felt. "I can't help feeling ashamed." The silence that followed made him nervous. What was Jamie thinking? Was she ashamed of him too? Knowing he might not like the expression he saw, Whit looked in her direction. She stood with her eyes fixed on the building across the street, the scarf blocking her profile. When she finally spoke, it was with care. "Frankie Johnson, the athlete I worked with, said something to me when we were writing his book last year and the words stuck with me. He said, 'If I hadn't messed up as spectacularly as I did, I wouldn't be the man I am today. It's not the failing that defines me; it's the getting back up.'"

"Did he really say that?"

"More or less. I might have tweaked the words a little bit." She looked at him with what he swore was encouragement. "What I'm saying is, look at everything you're doing with your foundation— all the programs you have planned. None of them would exist if you hadn't battled your own problems."

"I'm hardly inventing the wheel here. There are many other organizations tackling these issues. Even if I never came along with my foundation, someone else would have," he said.

"Maybe, but you're the one shaping its vision today." Her hand gripped his shoulder, fingers squeezing firm through the padding in an effort to be felt. "Give yourself some credit, Whit. No matter how weak you think you were, remember that you battled back, and that takes extraordinary strength."

She wouldn't be offering encouragement if she knew how badly he'd screwed up, that his so-called strength had come at the expense of another person.

There would be plenty of time to tear himself down later, however. For the moment, he decided to let her words stand.

Reaching up, he entwined his fingers with hers. The yarn of her gloves felt coarse in the cold, but the contact soothed him, nonetheless. "You always did see me as something better than I was."

"Maybe," she murmured. "Or..." He felt her lean closer, and her breath brushed the skin beneath his ear. "Maybe I'm seeing you as you really are."

Whit let her words wash over him, wondering if she knew how much they affected him.

Maybe, he thought, he was the one seeing things more clearly now. Maybe he hadn't appreciated just how lucky he'd been when they were dating.

"Thank you," he said, turning around.

"For what? I didn't do anything special."

Unwilling to break the connection quite yet, he kept their hands joined. His agitation with himself faded. It was too easy to feel comfortable when he was in Jamie's presence. "You listened to me," he told her.

"I'm supposed to listen to you; it's my job."

"Up here it's not. You didn't have to listen to a word I said if you didn't want to, and you sure as hell didn't have to try to reassure me."

The shadows might hide her cheek color, but the way she ducked her head exposed her. She was blushing. "Whit…"

"Shh. Just take the compliment, will you?"

He leaned in and kissed her on the cheek.

When he pulled back, Jamie's eyes were wide with brown-eyed wonder. Their sparkle in the dark sucker-punched him, bringing back all the warm, indescribable sensations he'd felt before. He wanted to kiss her properly. So badly it hurt.

And from the way her eyes were studying his mouth, she was thinking the same way.

She angled her head ever so slightly and leaned toward him.

"Jams," he whispered, the old, intimate nickname springing naturally to his lips.

Jamie froze. What was she thinking?

You were thinking you wanted to kiss him.

Now who felt ashamed? She'd taken a gesture of kindness and completely twisted it around. Her stomach felt like she might be sick.

"I—I think we should head inside," she stammered.

Whit was looking at her with an expression that looked like disappointment but was more likely confusion. Because she didn't feel quite embarrassed enough, he placed his hands on her shoulders.

"You're shivering," he said.

She managed to force a smile. "Wouldn't you if you were standing on a roof without pants on?"

"Why didn't you say something?" Without another word, he propelled her toward the door, his hand having moved from her shoulder to the small of her back. He opened the door, and they stepped into the warm stairwell. "You must be hungry too," he said.

"Not really." She suspected the next thing he said would be a dinner invitation, which was out of the question. Whit would probably pick some charming Manhattan bistro where they'd share a small table under dim lights. The notion was far too appealing.

"It's been a long day," she continued. "If you don't mind, I'm going to order in and go to bed early."

"Sure. Of course. If that's what you want. We can always grab dinner tomorrow."

"Exactly," she said. Or grab nothing at all. They could simply do their interview and part ways. "Tomorrow will be a completely different day."

Tomorrow was a different day all right. One that came with very little sleep. Jamie had always thought the whole "reliving the romantic moment, sleepless night" thing was an overused trope. Turned out it was a trope for a reason. It took her forever to fall asleep. Every time she closed her eyes, she returned to the rooftop, only instead of her backing away, she finished the kiss. Her imagination supplied every detail. The coolness of his lips, the warmth of his tongue. She could even smell his aftershave, thanks to Whit's good-night hug. Another friendly gesture that left her melting. She couldn't help herself.

"Told you so." Keisha's voice sounded loud in her head.

"It's sexual attraction. Big difference," she argued out loud. Hardly a shock seeing as she hadn't had sex for over two years and Whit was a known commodity, practically oozing with virility. What semi-celibate woman wouldn't want to kiss him? Or let him take her on the rooftop?

Her imagination went there too.

Didn't matter what her best friend's voice said, she wasn't unearthing emotions she'd long since buried. They may be lurking closer to the surface than she'd like, but they were staying well and truly buried. The only reason they were here together right now was that he needed her writing talents. Once the project ended, so would their relationship. She refused to cry over his leaving her for a second time in her life.

She was in the shower scrubbing off her fantasies when the phone rang. Grabbing her towel, she quickly wrapped it around he, before snatching the phone off the vanity.

"Please tell me I didn't wake you?" With seven words, Whit's honeyed voice undid everything the shower had accomplished. Suddenly, a towel was inadequate.

"Ha-ha," she said as she reached into the closet for the complimentary robe. "It just so happens I've been awake for hours." Because her dreams woke her up, but that was beside the point.

"You sleep all right then? The room is comfortable enough?"

"The room is amazing." A corner suite with two walls dedicated to windows overlooking the city. If she hadn't feared the view would add to her fantasies, Jamie would have left open the blinds and watched the skyline from her bed. "A regular room would have been fine."

"Regular New York hotel rooms are small. I wanted you to be comfortable while you were here."

Comfortable? She felt positively pampered.

"Have you looked outside yet this morning?" Whit asked.

"No, why?"

"Take a look. I'll wait."

Jamie yanked back the curtain and gasped. "Snow!" Outside her window, the air was filled with fluffy white flakes. They drifted lazily to the ground below. It looked like a winter wonderland.

"Forecast predicts we will get a couple inches," Whit said. "Most of it will be melted by tomorrow, I'm afraid."

In the meantime, the world looked beautiful. When she was a little girl, Jamie thought days like these were magical. "I've always loved snowy days," she said.

"I know. I remember how excited you were when we had that snow day at college. You wanted to go build a snowman."

"And you convinced me to stay in bed."

"Hey! I don't remember you complaining at the time."

Thank goodness they were on the phone and he couldn't see her face. Jamie remembered that snow day. The two of them had spent twenty-four hours naked and wrapped around each other.

"Anyway," he continued, "seeing as how I've got a chance for a do-over, I'm declaring today a snow day."

Jamie frowned. "Snow day, like in canceling work? What about the story?"

"The story can wait another twenty-four hours."

Ahh, now she understood. This wasn't about a do-over. This was about avoiding an uncomfortable topic. "Sooner or later, you're going to have to tell me the bad stuff you keep alluding to. You can't tell a cautionary tale without sharing everything."

"I know," he replied, "and I promise you will hear my sad, sordid tale soon enough. But today is a beautiful snowy day, and I want to show you New York in the snow. We can go ice skating in Central Park. Have you ever seen the park in the snow?"

No, but she could imagine how beautiful the snow-covered trees must look. Still, it was a bad idea. What he was describing sounded too much like a date, which, after last night, was the last thing her imagination needed. "We really should be working," she told him.

"Come on. When is the last time you had fun?"

"What are you talking about? I have fun."

"Doing what?" he asked. "Game night? Going out for drinks with Kish? You told me yourself that you spend most of your time working and don't have a lot of time to play around. Wouldn't you like to laugh a little? God knows I would." His voice dropped a notch and developed a pleading note. "Say yes, Jams. I promise I'll answer every question you ask tomorrow, but I need a day off."

How could she say no when he phrased it like that? She looked out at the giant white flakes floating down like the petals falling from a tree. When was the last time she'd really laughed? Probably with Keisha somewhere, but if she couldn't remember, it must not have been that memorable. Maybe a day off wasn't such a bad idea. A relaxed subject was always more animated and talkative. During the course of the day she could weave in a few questions and, maybe, get some good background information.

That's right, she was doing this for the article, not because ice skating in the park with Whit sounded romantically awesome.

"All right," she told him. "We'll take a day off."

"I'll pick you up in an hour. Dress warm."

Jamie clicked off the phone. Immediately, butterflies took flight in her stomach. *Deep breaths, Jams.* This was no different than shadowing a business subject. Two people hanging out for the day. There was absolutely no reason to wig out.

Who was she kidding? She was totally wigging out.

CHAPTER SIX

WHIT HUNG UP the phone with a smile. Mission accomplished.

As soon as he saw the snow, he knew he had to drag Jamie to Central Park. That snow day from years ago popped into his head along with her childlike enthusiasm. Being a twenty-one-year-old male at the time, he'd preferred indoor sports to making a snowman and had proceeded to demonstrate why.

It had been a great day.

Today there would be no "indoor sports," although the memories of the one they'd shared did enter his mind—vividly too. While he might not be twenty-one anymore, he was male, a fact he seemed to be more and more aware of whenever he was near Jamie.

Today, though, really was about having fun. If, by doing so, he also postponed talking about Capri, then so what? One day more wouldn't hurt anything.

Plus, he meant what he'd said about needing to laugh. Since the day he'd entered the rehab clinic, he'd been focused on atonement. Was it wrong to want just a few hours when he didn't feel the guilt pressing down on his shoulders?

Then there was Jamie. She who was "too busy working" to have any kind of social life. Wouldn't hurt her to take a day off either. And besides, he owed her a little lightness for making her listen to his dark stories. Seemed like all he did was take from her—her skills, her comfort, her soothing presence. It was selfish of him, he knew, but damn, she made him feel good.

What would his life have been like if he'd stayed in the States instead of going to Europe? If Jamie had given him some kind of indication that she'd wanted him to stay, would he have been tempted to tear up his polo contract?

He didn't know. But the question was moot anyway. It was all water under the bridge, he thought with a sigh. You couldn't change the past. As for the present…? Who'd want a relationship with someone with his baggage?

He shook away the dark thoughts. Today was about enjoying themselves. He planned to make it a day Jamie would remember.

Exactly fifty-five minutes after their call ended, Whit walked into the St. Pierre lobby. He arrived just as Jamie emerged from the elevator, dressed for the elements. No stocking-clad legs today. Her long coat was unbuttoned, revealing jeans and an oversized fisherman's sweater. Her hair was twisted in another one of those messy top knots with wisps already falling loose. Even in casual clothes, she was the nicest looking part of the luxury lobby. A spot of brightness amid dark wood and steel.

He caught her eye only to have her look down as she tucked a strand of hair behind her ear. Like a girl on a first date. The idea she was feeling shy and self-conscious made his pulse stutter. Was it possible she'd been as moved by their closeness last night as he'd been? All of a sudden, the air crackled with expectancy.

"Good morning!" He held out one of the green-and-white paper cups he held in his hands. "I brought coffee. Medium black and white."

Her eyes widened. "Oh, my God, I haven't ordered one of those in years. I can't believe you even remembered it."

"How could I forget? Whenever we went to Café Nomad, you insisted on ordering off the 'secret menu.'"

"That was a Keisha influence. We thought ordering an off-menu coffee made us look sophisticated. These days I'm more interested in getting in and out of the coffee shop as fast as possible. Time is money and all, right?" she quipped as she took the cup. "Thank you."

"You're welcome." He knew she was making a joke, but her comment about time and money saddened him.

In fact, several of her comments saddened him. Ever since their conversation in the Map Room. It was as if she'd lost her fanciful side. Maybe she'd simply grown older and become more practical; Lord knows if he'd grown up, she must have too. But he couldn't shake the feeling in his gut saying there was something else wrong here. Which made him doubly glad he was dragging her along on his snow day today.

"This is delicious," she told him. "I'd forgotten just how good steamed milk could taste."

There was a line of foam on her upper lip. Whit tried not to stare as the tip of her tongue flicked it away.

"Glad you're enjoying the treat," he said before taking a sip of his own black coffee. "Are you ready to tackle the ice-skating rink?"

"I think so. Been a while since I've worn skates, though."

"Good. Me too. Means we'll be on an equal footing."

"Or lack of," she replied. "Hope you have a plan for when we bruise our behinds falling down all the time."

He hadn't, but now that she'd said something, an idea was forming in his head. A little out there maybe, but then, this wasn't a first date. It was two friends hanging out.

"Shall we?" Out of habit, he started to hold

out his elbow, but he quickly caught himself and waved for her to walk ahead instead.

"Not yet. I need to cover my head," she told him. She reached into her pocket and pulled out a long red scarf.

Whit smiled. In last night's hurried and awkward goodbye, he'd completely forgotten about retrieving his scarf.

"I meant to return this today," she told him, "but seeing as how we're going out in the snow and I didn't pack a hat, can I borrow it again?"

"Looks better on you than me anyway." He held her coffee while she wrapped the cashmere over her head. For a second Whit was thrust back to the night before and the arresting image of her moonlit face. Once again, that odd sense of fullness gripped his chest. There was a loose tendril on her cheek. He reached out and tucked it gently into the scarf. "Now you're ready to go," he said.

Well, she was managing things well, wasn't she? Less than five minutes into the day and her knees had already nearly buckled. Why on earth did she put on Whit's scarf? The plan was to buy a hat in one of the city's four zillion gift shops and give back his amazingly soft, bay-rum-scented piece of material. Then she'd pulled the thing from her pocket and poof! The plan went right out of her head. Meanwhile her heart did a little bounce when he smiled at her. Keep this up, and she was in for a long day.

The two of them stepped out onto Madison Avenue. Snow continued to fall gently. Jamie looked down at the sidewalk, surprised to find less than an inch on the ground.

"Perfect kind of snow," Whit remarked. "Looks gorgeous but doesn't hang around. By tomorrow you'll never even know it snowed."

Looking at the fluffy white curtain, it was hard to believe.

"Central Park is only a few blocks from here," he said. "Would you rather ride or walk?"

"Do you mind if we walk?"

"Not at all." A familiar black car was idling near the curb. Whit knocked on the window, signaling the driver to lower the glass. "The lady prefers to walk," he told him. "We'll call when we need you." As they headed down the street, Jamie couldn't help tilting her head back and looking up at the snowfall. Focusing on the weather kept her from thinking about the man at her elbow. "Makes you feel like you're walking in a snow globe, doesn't it?" she asked.

"Having never walked in a snow globe, I'll take your word for it. Only in this case, let's hope no one decides to shake us up because that would be an earthquake."

"Way to kill the metaphor, Martin."

"I try," he replied with a grin.

Cradling her coffee in her hands, Jamie used her two-handed grip to steal a look at Whit while sipping. Unlike her, he had brought a hat. A black watch cap that he pulled out of his pocket and jammed on his head. His wire glasses were spotted with droplets. A little longer in the cold and the tip of his nose would turn red too. He looked adorable.

And she'd better work on maintaining some emotional distance.

"Better enjoy your snow globe while you can. According to the radar, the snow is going to end in another hour," he told her. "The good news is we'll be skating in it."

"I didn't realize Central Park had ice skating," she said. When she thought about skating in New York City, she thought about Rockefeller Center or Bryant Library Park.

"Central Park has everything. You should know that."

She pressed a hand to her chest. "I humbly apologize. Is there a reason you picked this rink instead of the more famous ice rinks in this city?"

"Apology accepted, and everyone goes to Rockefeller Center and Bryant Park. This particular rink is smaller, but less crowded. A day like today we'll have the rink almost to ourselves."

Sounded lovely.

As they walked the last few blocks to the park, Whit told her about the Winter Carnival that was held in the park and had recently ended. "If there isn't enough snow, they'll make it special so there's enough for sledding and other activities," he said. "You'll get to see some of the ice sculptures too. The cold weather means there hasn't been a lot of melting."

"Reminds me of those events they hold at the local ski slopes," Jamie said. "Without the skiing, of course."

"It's pretty popular, especially with families. What little kid wouldn't want to go sledding?"

"Did you go?" Soon as she asked, Jamie suspected the answer.

"The nanny took me a couple times. Most of the time we went to the park near our building. There was a sledding hill there."

Jamie was relieved by his answer. After everything Whit had revealed about his younger years, there was a part of her that worried he'd missed out on a lot of basic childhood pleasures. "This must have been before your troublemaking days with your cousin," she noted.

"Way before. Different nanny as well. This one left to get married when I was six or seven."

"How many nannies did you have?"

"Three, although the last one was more of an expensive babysitter. Probably very expensive since I was in my tween years by then." He frowned. "What is it?"

"Nothing, really," Jamie replied. "The way you toss around terms like *nanny* and *polo*. Sometimes it hits me how vastly different our worlds are."

He looked her straight on. "Different, but one isn't necessarily better," he said.

"I know," Jamie said quietly. Stealing another look at his profile, which had grown sober, Jamie regretted saying anything. It was one of those times when the sheer volume of Whit's wealth struck her full force. In college, Whit's money had meant little to her. In fact, other than teasing him about the Martin Science Center on campus, she'd hardly thought about his family's money. His other qualities—his looks, his charisma, his popularity—those were what had overwhelmed her. The last few days, however, had reminded her that being a Martin carried its own special baggage. She'd never truly appreciated that before.

They crossed Fifth Avenue onto the Grand Army Plaza with its gold statue of William Tecumseh Sherman and hurried past the cars to the park entrance.

Jamie stopped short and stared at the tree-lined sidewalks. With their branches bowed under the weight of the snow, the treetops joined together to form a winter canopy. Everything, the trees, the sky, the walkway—was in shades of black and gray. The effect was otherworldly.

"This only happens a few times a year," Whit said, "but when it does, it's spectacular."

"Almost like someone waved a wand and sucked the color out of the air." She looked over at him. "You're smiling. What is it?"

"I like your description," he replied. "You have a way with words."

"So I've been told." The compliment felt grander than it was because of her surroundings. She looked around for signs, but the words were covered with snow. "Which way to the rink?"

"Up and to the left," Whit replied. "There's actually two rinks, but this one's the closest."

As they headed down the nearly empty walkway, Jamie kept her face turned upward. Her face was getting wet, but she didn't care. The surroundings were too beautiful. "Is this when you tell me you took figure skating lessons or played semi-pro ice hockey?" Because it wouldn't surprise her.

"Well, I do perform a mean triple Lutz. Just kidding," he said when she whipped her head around. "No skating lessons or ice hockey, I swear."

"Good, because when I said I hadn't been ice skating in ages, I meant ages. Last time I put on skates was when I was thirteen and I was rudimentary at best. Which means that not only won't you see triple Lutzes from me, you'll be lucky if you see me stay up period. Graceful, I am not."

She was talking to herself. "Whit?"

"Smile."

She turned around to find him holding his phone. "I couldn't resist," he said. "The scarf and the trees made too good a photo. Want to see?"

He held the camera out as he walked toward her. The picture on the screen was of her in the center of the walkway, snow covering her shoulders and head, looking surprised while the trees bent behind her. Amid all the gray and white, her red scarf appeared to glow.

"Not bad if I do say so myself," he said.

"Are you kidding? I look like a snow-covered waif."

"Nonsense. You look fantastic. The best-looking snow-covered waif in the city. Come closer and we'll take a selfie."

Jamie did as she was told, leaning into the crook of his shoulder as he snapped several shots. She tried not to think about how warm his body felt despite the cold or how closely their cheeks were to one another.

When he'd finished, Whit lowered his arm, but made no move to increase the space between their bodies. On the screen, their faces smiled back at them in the snow. "There. Now we have a record of the day."

Even with the water marking his glasses, Jamie could see his hooded eyes. His gaze caressed her cheeks.

Cold air struck her side where he'd been standing. "Skating," he said.

Right. Skating. Releasing the breath she'd been holding, Jamie turned around and followed him toward the rink. He certainly wasn't making her emotional distance vow easy, was he? Fortunately, while they were skating, she'd be too busy trying to stay upright to let him distract her.

No one could say Jamie undersold her skating prowess. She could skate—forward—but couldn't quite make the stopping part work. Instead she would skate in one direction and when she wanted to stop, drag the front of her blade until she slowed down. Frequently this resulted in her losing balance and either catching herself with her hand or landing on her bottom.

He was only moderately better, Whit realized, because he knew how to stop. The two of them were the oldest and worst skaters on the rink. Toddlers pushing milk crates outskated them. After two hours, his back was bothering him, and his cheeks hurt from grinning. That was Jamie's doing. She embraced her lack of grace with enthusiasm, her laugh ringing out every time she stumbled or fell. The sound was infectious. How could he not embrace the moment and laugh too?

"That," he said, once they handed in their skates, "was an experience. I think it's safe to say no one will be recruiting us for the Olympics anytime soon."

Jamie let out a laugh. "Don't count me out yet, Mr. Triple Lutz. I learned how to stop today."

"Your teacher was five years old, and he asked if you needed a milk crate." Whit had howled at the offer.

"Still counts," she said pertly. "Didn't see you learning a new skill."

But she was wrong. He'd learned how to have a silly, outrageous time while stone cold sober. Damn, but it felt good.

And he did it all while behaving like a perfect gentleman. After last night's almost slip, he wanted to make sure Jamie didn't think he had ulterior motives in spending the day with her. Therefore, there were no shoulder nudges or hands on her waist. When she fell, he offered a hand up, but nothing more. He completely ignored the desire to wrap his arms around her that had been eating at him since he took her picture.

Jamie didn't need to know any of that, however. "Thank you for playing hooky with me," he told her. "I needed this."

"Thank you for inviting me," she replied. "I had fun."

Whit smiled. "Never would have guessed from the laughing."

The snow had stopped while they were skating. Jamie had slipped the scarf from her head and let the material drape around her neck in a cowl. Her hair was messier than ever from all the activity. Strands fell around her face in soft wisps, while the topknot drooped to the side. It reminded him of how she used to look after she'd been sleeping.

He watched, intrigued as she untwisted and then re-twisted the bun without looking. The result was neater, but still tousled. Whit got the itch to pull everything free and comb it with his fingers. He jammed his fingers in his pockets.

"What should we do next?" he asked.

"It's your snow day. What would you like to do?"

"Good question. Something that is a little easier on my back, perhaps. I tweaked it when I was attempting to skate backwards."

Concern filled her eyes. "I'm sorry. Does it hurt a lot?"

Didn't hurt at all when she looked at him like that. "Nothing a hot shower before bed can't cure." Or a soak in a mineral bath. He was starting to get an idea.

"Look, the zoo is open," Jamie suddenly said,

pointing to the gate ahead. "I didn't know you could visit the zoo in the winter."

"Absolutely. Zoo's open year-round. Some of the animals are cold weather animals."

"Let's go," she said.

She was kidding, right? The sparkle in her eyes said she wasn't. "I haven't been to the zoo since I was a little kid," he said.

"You hadn't been skating since you were little either. Didn't stop you from strapping blades on your feet."

No, it did not. He thought about the idea he'd had and then looked at the woman in front of him with her windblown cheeks and messy hair. Her eyes were bright with excitement.

"You really want to visit the zoo, don't you?" he asked.

"Yes, I do," she replied enthusiastically. "If you'd like, I'll even buy the tickets."

How could he resist a face that lovely? His idea could wait an hour or so. "All right, let's go look at animals."

His reward was a smile so radiant it could melt snow. "You're going to love it," she promised.

He already was. Once they had paid their admission—they compromised by each buying their own ticket—he retreated to an overhang near the public restrooms.

"Go ahead and I'll catch up," he told her, pulling his phone out of a pocket. "I'm going to arrange for the car to pick us up."

"Do you plan on being too cold to walk?"

"Something like that," he said. The car also made executing his surprise much easier. As his thumb hovered over the keypad, he wondered if, in this particular case, surprising Jamie was the best idea. His idea did have an element of awkwardness attached to it. On the other hand, if he told her about it, she'd probably say no straight out, and he was positive that once she relaxed, she would enjoy herself.

He dialed. What was the worst that could happen? She refused to get out of the car, and they drove back to the hotel? Call it a crazy hunch, but he didn't think that would be the case.

Having made his arrangements, he hurried down the path to the zoo center, where Jamie stood watching the snow monkeys soaking in their man-made hot spring. She pointed to the two largest monkeys, who sat chin deep. Steam rose off the water around them. "They look comfortable, don't they?" Whit contemplated the pair's wizened faces. Their eyes blinked in sleepy contentment as they sat in total indifference to their audience. "The Japanese macaque, also known as the snow monkey, can be found in Honshu, Japan." He read off a nearby sign. "Says here they have very strict social rankings, with the monkeys at the highest tiers receiving the most grooming. That means, if we apply the same standard to humans..."

She cut him off. "You can pick off your own nits."

"Don't be so quick to shoot it down. I'm not the one with thick hair." Unable to help himself, he broke his rule and pretended to pick at her hair, earning a playful hand slap.

"Keep your hands to yourself, Martin." The admonition, however, was said with a smile.

Turned out Jamie was right about the zoo. Whit did enjoy himself. For an hour they explored the various exhibits, laughing as the penguins and sea lions performed for attention, and marveling at the majesty of the snow leopard.

"You remind me of a snow leopard," Jamie said as they watched the cat stretch out on a heated ledge.

"Really?" Surprised him to hear her say so. A fluffy white wildcat was the last animal he'd compare himself to. "How so?"

"Look at him. He doesn't have to do a thing and yet everyone knows he's at the top of the food chain. There isn't even an argument."

Whit looked at her. "Is that how you see me?"

"It's presence," she continued, not answering his question. "If that leopard morphed into a house cat tomorrow, he'd still radiate superiority."

She turned her face toward him. "As would you."

"I'm flattered." More than flattered, since it meant she'd been paying him close attention.

"Don't be," she said, giving a shrug. "I'm only stating a fact."

Sounded like more than a fact to him, especially when she looked at him with eyes the color of brown velvet. When he looked into them, the earth tipped a little.

"Well, if we're making animal comparisons, you are the red panda."

"Mild mannered and sleeps the day away?"

"Adorable and rare," he replied. He kissed the tip of her nose with his finger.

Just as he hoped, she dipped her head. God, he loved when she blushed.

"There's only one problem," she said as she looked up through her lashes. "Snow leopards eat red pandas."

Did they? Whit wasn't so sure. Considering the way he felt at the moment, he was pretty sure the red panda could wrap the snow leopard around its little finger.

"All right, I admit it. I'm glad we don't have to walk back to the hotel." Jamie lay her head back on the headrest and reveled in the warm air blowing up her pants leg. Snowy days were wonderful, but they were also cold.

The aroma of warm chocolate and hazelnut filled the backseat. On the way out, Whit had stopped to buy gourmet hot cocoa along with a stuffed red panda that he insisted she have. "As a souvenir," he said. The toy rested on the seat between them.

She wondered if her leopard comparison had been a good idea. It was the truth though. Whit could be a ditch digger and people would cede to his authority. Given the shame that unscored many of his remarks, she figured he could use the reminder. She wasn't expecting him to make a comparison back or call her rare. Every time she repeated the word in her head, she fluttered.

"Ready for one more adventure?" Whit asked. He shifted so that he faced her.

"Depends," she replied cautiously. "What do you have in mind?" The fluttering went into overdrive as she conjured up several scenarios. All of them, she was ashamed to admit, involving Whit kissing her.

"Nothing too dangerous, I promise."

His arm was stretched across the back of the seat. She could sense the cuff of his sleeve as it lay near her shoulder. The position managed to encapsulate the entire day. All day long Jamie had been acutely aware of Whit's physical proximity to her. After tucking the hair behind her ear at the hotel, he'd kept a nice, respectable distance from her. No shoulder bumps, no guiding hand on the small of back or accidental brush of his arm against hers. In fact, she could count the number of times they'd made physical contact on one hand, and one was pretending to pick bugs out of her hair. It was what she'd wanted: physical and emotional distance.

It was also driving her crazy. There were moments when she'd caught herself trying to force a touch. Her brain asked question after question, seeking an explanation. Had she embarrassed herself last night? Was he afraid she might get the wrong impression and was trying to avoid giving her mixed signals? If so, he might want to tone down the charm and stop using words like *adorable* and *rare* to describe her.

The reason for this sudden obsession she likened to eating on a diet. When you were told to lay off junk food, all you could think about were the ice cream bars in the freezer.

The urge for physical contact began creeping in anew now that they were sitting next to each other on the back seat of the car and discussing *adventures*—another word that should be avoided. "Do I get a hint?" she asked.

"About the adventure?" He shifted his weight again, bringing his arm closer. "Remember right before we went to the zoo when you asked me what I wanted to do? This is it."

"That's not a hint."

"You'll get nice and warm while we're there." Leaning in, he added, "You might even sweat a little."

"We're going to a Zumba class?"

Whit started laughing. His laugh was a great sound, full-bodied and hearty. Jamie felt a ripple of pleasure every time she heard it because it meant Whit was genuinely relaxed. She enjoyed seeing him happy and at ease. Made for an easier interview, she told herself, despite the fact she had yet to ask him any real questions. Their talk about sledding didn't count. The conversation merely added to what she already knew about Whit's childhood. It had been lonely.

Turning away from Whit, Jamie looked out the window, hoping a landmark might give her a clue. Nothing looked familiar except the gift shops. Every block had similar-looking store fronts displaying the same New York souvenirs.

"And, we're here," Whit announced.

CHAPTER SEVEN

THEY HAD STOPPED in front of a double storefront whose white facade was decorated with large columns. The sign over the front door swung in the breeze. Clumps of snow partially obscured the letters, but Jamie could make out the word *Bath*.

"You took me to a bathhouse?" Every ounce of her pleasant mood threatened to vanish as she pictured soaking up steam while surrounded by an abundance of towel-wrapped men, only one of which was built like Whit. "That's not an adventure. That's…"

"Not a bathhouse," Whit replied. "It's a Roman bath spa. Here, take a look."

On his phone, Whit had called up the spa's website. Jamie read the home page, which promised customers' tensions would "melt away" as they relaxed "in one of the spa's seven mineral pools inspired by the famed baths of the Roman empire."

"It's like sitting in a hot tub, only bigger and with better water. A session in one of these and all those bumps and bruises you got from skating will fade away."

Reading the description, Jamie had to admit, it sounded tempting. She had envied the snow monkeys sitting in their hot tub. But after last night's fantasies, did she really want to sit in warm, steaming water while Whit and his bare torso sat on the other side?

"I don't have a bathing suit," she pointed out.

"Not a problem. I called ahead and explained. They're setting aside a couple suits from the gift shop for us."

Of course he did.

"Look," he continued. "I thought a soak would be good for my back and that you might appreciate soaking your aching muscles too, but not if it's going to make you feel awkward. I'll have Lars take you back to the hotel."

"You don't have to," Jamie said. She was being silly. The baths were at least eight or nine feet long. How was soaking in one in a bathing suit any different from sitting in a hotel hot tub? "It looks like fun."

If she was having trouble controlling her attraction to him, that was her problem, not his.

"Do you need a different size suit?" The woman on the other side of the dressing room door had a voice as smooth as silk. Soft like silk too. Exactly the kind of voice you'd want to hear in a spa. Jamie wondered if that was a prerequisite for the job.

By contrast, her own voice sounded loud. "No thank you," she said. "This one fits."

Someone, either Whit or the woman with the lovely voice, did a good job of selecting the size. The plain black suit was neither sexy nor overly modest. There was a small V in the front and a plunging back.

The spa itself was nothing like she'd imagined, although given she'd imagined a stereotypical bathhouse sauna, that wasn't too hard. Everything was soft and soothing as the spa associate's voice. Hints of lavender and salt infused the air, mingling with the low sounds of ambient music. When Jamie stepped out of the dressing room, it was into a softly lit locker room with vanity mirrors and heated floors.

The associate handed her a thick white towel and a pair of bamboo sandals. "The bath area is through the door at the end of the corridor. Enjoy your experience."

Experience was definitely a good way to put it. Feeling exposed wearing only a bathing suit, Jamie wrapped the towel around her midsection. As she walked down the hall, listening to the loud clapping of the sandals against her feet, she was again struck by the quiet. It wasn't just the ambiance. There was an atmosphere of privacy, like she was the only person in the building. She hadn't even heard or seen Whit. He'd disappeared down the men's corridor shortly after their arrival.

Jamie winced as the door latch clicked loudly

upon opening. All these noises felt like an intrusion on the tranquility. She imagined every head in the room turning to see who'd caused the disruption. Slowly opening the door, she stepped inside prepared to apologize, and instead let out an audible gasp.

She was standing in a Roman bath. An honest-to-God ancient bath, or more accurately a replica of one. The entire room had been transformed into a cavern, the dark "rock" walls streaked with copper and blue. While there were small spotlights placed around the space, most of the light came from the pools themselves. Seven ten-foot rectangles were laid out perpendicular to a long lap pool.

Whit was already sitting in the center pool, arms stretched out across the rim, his body submerged to his breastbone. Upon seeing her, he gestured with his head. "You going to stand there gawking or are you getting in?"

"This place is unbelievable. How on earth did you find it?"

"I've come here a couple times when I needed to unwind."

"What about the rooftop? I thought that was your quiet place?"

"The rooftop doesn't have the same effect on my bad back."

A fair argument. She took off the towel and

folded it neatly. It was silly to feel nervous about letting Whit see her in a bathing suit, considering the man had seen her naked, but she was. Seven years was a long time. Jamie liked to think her body hadn't changed too much, but that didn't mean Whit would agree or that he'd like what he saw. It was strictly vanity that had her hoping he would.

She needn't have worried. When she turned around, Whit's eyes were glittering with obvious appreciation. "Suit looks good on you," he said.

"You aren't wearing your glasses," she retorted. Nevertheless, a rush of self-satisfaction ran through her.

"I can see well enough. Stairs are over there." He nodded.

Whit was right. Slipping into the water was like slipping into a piece of heaven. Jamie let out a sigh as muscles she didn't even know were tense began to relax. "Much better than a hot tub. This is addictive." She cringed. "Sorry. Bad choice of words."

"Actually, I'd say an accurate choice. You don't have to censor yourself, Jams. It's only a word."

"I just don't want to make you feel uncomfortable."

"You won't. If anything…"

"What?" she asked. Wasn't fair to leave her hanging in midsentence.

"If anything, I've been more comfortable the past few days than I have in a long time."

Oh, wow. Jamie swallowed down the feelings rising inside her. Statements like that, coupled with sincere blue eyes, were made to melt a girl's heart. When he said stuff like that, it was hard for her to remember their romance had ended seven years ago. They were merely friends and colleagues now.

Since she didn't trust herself to respond without stumbling into trouble, she changed the topic. The cavern was noticeably empty. "Your favorite spa doesn't seem too popular with others," she noted. "Or did we simply come at a slow time?"

"Middle of the workday is usually slow."

There was a *but* to his answer. She could tell from the way his gaze dropped to the water before answering. A sure sign of avoidance. What was he avoiding regarding the spa's business traffic?

Suddenly it hit her. Why they had the entire spa to themselves. "Please tell me you didn't," she said, slightly horrified.

There was no need to tell her; the look he gave her defined sheepish.

"You booked out the entire spa?"

"I thought you'd appreciate the privacy."

"*I* would appreciate it, or *you* would appreciate it?" she asked.

"Maybe a little bit of both?" he offered. Jamie narrowed her eyes. "All right, the truth is, I figured I owed you a grand gesture. All those months we dated in college and the fanciest thing we did was go out to dinner before the Senior Ball."

"We didn't do anything fancy because I didn't need to," she protested. All she had needed was his company.

"I know, but you're the kind of girl who deserves at least one. So, here you go."

Jamie's heart was struggling not to melt again, but damn, he didn't make things easy. She shook her head to clear the tears dampening her eyes. "You're unbelievable."

His eyes reached across the pool to hold hers. "My pleasure."

They sat and soaked in silence for a while, content to listen to the music and let the water wash everything else away. While she sat, Jamie used the time to get her emotions under control. Wasn't every day someone made a grand romantic gesture on her behalf. This was the kind of thing she'd fantasized about when she was in school. When you were a teenager, or barely past, you believed such fantasies might be possible. Breaking up with Whit had made her grow up quickly and shelve those stupid notions. And now here he was, making them come alive again. In fact, this entire day, she'd felt like her college-aged self. It was a dangerous feeling because with her old self came old feelings.

Her thoughts were disrupted by a soft splash. She opened her eyes to find that Whit had left the bath and dived into the lap pool. His arms rose and fell in even strokes as he moved from one end to the other and back. After a handful of passes, he swam to the side, where he hung on the edge. "Needed a cooldown," he remarked. "I was afraid I'd fall asleep."

She knew what he meant. Her own body was feeling comfortably drowsy, which probably wasn't the best thing in a hot tub. Much as she didn't want to, Jamie pushed herself to her feet. "Is the water cold?" she asked.

"Not really. Feels brisk at first, but then you get used to it. Come on in, I'll race you." With that, he pushed himself back to the middle of the pool.

By the time Jamie had climbed out of the mineral bath and made her way to the pool, Whit had resumed swimming laps. He moved with the precision of a practiced swimmer. She watched with admiration as he kicked off each turn, his body gliding smoothly under the water. When he broke to the surface, it was with a burst of energy and strength. He moved from freestyle to the breaststroke to the butterfly, his shoulder muscles flexing with each downward slice of his arms.

Good Lord, he even swam with authority. It was a thing of beauty.

"Are you coming in?" he called from the far end of the pool.

What the hell. She was already drowning. Might as well get wet too.

"Can I ask you a question?" Whit asked.

"I don't know, can you?" Jamie replied. She tossed her head back and giggled, the sound floating through the cavern.

Whit laughed. The two of them were stretched out on their towels by the edge of the pool, relaxing after their swim. There was no rush to leave; he'd paid for the afternoon as well as extra sessions and massages for any customers displaced by his request. Thankfully the manager assured him they got very little afternoon traffic and only a handful of people were affected. Since returning, Whit had sworn off being one of "those" rich men who threw their money around and demanded special treatment. The people he used to party with were constantly guilty of it. Consequently, he associated the behavior with his darkest time.

But he'd done it today, all because he wanted to surprise the woman lying beside him. He hadn't started out planning to rent the entire facility. The idea had come to him spontaneously when he was talking with the associate. He wasn't sure why other than he really had wanted to leave her with a great memory. Something positive to balance all the dark stuff that was to come.

Maybe he'd wanted to see the affection in her eyes one last time before she thought less of him.

Right now, though, he wanted to talk about her. There had been questions nagging at him since they'd talked in the Map Room. He propped himself on his elbow so he could better look at her. "May I ask you a question? Is that better?"

"Yes, and ask away."

"Why haven't you written your novel yet?"

Based on the widening of her eyes, the question caught her off guard. "I told you. I have to work. Pay the bills. It's hard to fit a novel in when you're writing everyone else's."

"Is that really the reason?"

"What else would it be?" She rolled to her side until they were face-to-face. "For that matter, why do you care? I would think you'd want me to be focused on writing your book."

"I'm surprised, that's all. In college, you talked my ear off about writing a book. The way you talked, I figured you'd be one of those people who took a mindless job so they could focus on their art."

"That is a romantic fantasy," she replied bluntly. "I gave those up."

"I know," Whit said. And it made him sad.

Jamie's attention had dropped to her towel and a loose thread that had pulled free from the edging. He watched as her fingers plucked at it, over and over. "How come?" he asked.

Her fingers stilled. "Life," she replied. "When I was a kid, I had this fantastic dream of how my life would be when I graduated college. It was all very romantic. But afterwards…" She twisted the thread around her index finger and tugged it until it snapped. "Let's just say dreams and imagination are great, but eventually you have wake up and pay off your student loans."

That was all well and good, but there was still something missing here. The world was filled with stories of authors who worked day jobs while toiling away on their manuscripts at night. Why hadn't she done that?

Jamie shrugged when he asked. "It's not like I didn't try. I wrote bits and pieces of stuff, but everything sounded silly. In the end, it was much easier to write other people's stuff."

He frowned.

"I don't know," she added as she flopped back down. "Maybe the whole thing was nothing more than a pipe dream."

"It wasn't." The forlornness in her voice crushed him. He hated that she'd lost faith in her plans. Or maybe it was in herself. Didn't matter.

She was wrong to cast her plans aside. "You can do it. You just can't give up," he urged her.

"No offense, Whit, but why do you even care? We've only been back in each other's orbits for a few weeks. Why do you care so much about whether I do anything?"

"Because," he said. But the reason he'd thought would come easily to his lips didn't. Truth was, he didn't know why he was suddenly so invested in her writing. He just was. It mattered to him that she chased her dreams. That she be happy.

"Do you remember how you would talk about your plans for after graduation?" he asked her. "How you were going to live this fantastic life?"

"Don't remind me."

"You would get so animated. Made me jealous."

Jamie's eyes, which until this point were closed, flew open. She scrambled to a sitting position. "You were jealous of me?"

"Sure? Why wouldn't I be? Pipe dream or not, at least you had a plan of your own. I was rudderless in comparison."

"No, you weren't."

"Yes, I was. For crying out loud, I ran away to Europe because I didn't have a proper plan for my life in the long term." Letting out a long breath, Whit sat up as well. This kind of conversation was best had face-to-face.

"I didn't know what I wanted to do. I only knew

I didn't want to keep following my grandfather's path, but beyond that…" Was it any wonder he'd fallen into a downward spiral like he had? "You, though. You were a dreamer. You saw the world through big, rose-colored glasses."

At the time, it had overwhelmed him, her fancifulness. There were times when, while talking, her eyes would glow with excitement, their color a mosaic of browns and golds, and Whit would have to remind himself to pull back before he was sucked into their spell.

"Problem is," Jamie said quietly, "rose-colored glasses aren't very realistic."

"Screw realistic," he said. "The world has plenty of realistic people."

Suddenly he realized what today had been all about. The park, the grand gesture. He was trying to return those rose-colored glasses to her. "People like you make the world unique, Jams," he told her. He hadn't properly appreciated her distinctiveness seven years ago, but he did today. "You believe in possibilities the rest of us don't see."

"Wow. You don't hold back when giving a compliment, do you?"

"Not when it's the truth. Hey," he said, urging her to look him in the eye, "you dreamed of attending a top-tier college and made that come true. Who says you can't make everything else come true too?"

* * *

For a man who refused to touch her, Whit was very good at coaxing a physical response from her. Jamie blinked back tears for the second time that day. "You have an awful lot of faith in me," she said.

"Of course, I do. I dated you, remember? And I only date the best."

He just didn't fall in love with any of them. *See*, she wanted to say, *some dreams don't come true*. But she didn't. Her heart was too full of emotion from his pep talk.

"Thank you," she said huskily. "I don't mean for the talk; I mean for everything. This entire day has been…unbelievable." To hell with distance, she reached across and rested her hand on his. "One I'm not likely to forget for a very long time."

"You're welcome." As he spoke, Whit flipped his hand over and pressed their palms together. The connection felt more intimate than it should. Like they belonged together. Always linked. Jamie wondered what would happen if she lay back and pulled Whit to her.

"I think I need another swim," Whit said abruptly. His hand slipped from her grip as he rose to his feet. Jamie pressed her hand to her abdomen to quell the needy ache. If there was such a thing as an imaginary precipice, then she was standing on its edge. She'd better be sure to leave her heart behind should she decide to tumble over. Because if she didn't, there was a good chance it wouldn't ever bounce back.

It was dark when they left the spa and took the car back to the hotel. Jamie leaned her head against the leather headrest, her body reveling in a delightfully liquid feeling. It was a little like being drunk. She rolled her head to the side to find Whit sitting in a similar position, the same contented smile on his face. Neither of them moved.

As the car crawled through the rush hour traffic, they kept their eyes on one another. The atmosphere had shifted during their time in the spa. The hum in the air was louder than it had been before. She could feel Whit's eyes exploring her body. He was touching her without touching, each pass of his gaze like a caress. Her body longed to slide across the seat and press against him, but the rest of her was too uncertain. *Damn it, touch me*, she thought. *Make the first move. Take the decision out of my hands.*

"It's almost dinner time." His voice floated across the seat. "Should I make reservations?"

Jamie shook her head. After everything, she was afraid having dinner with him might be more than she could handle. "Rain check?"

"Sure thing," he replied. The emotion crossing his face could have been disappointment, but Jamie wasn't sure.

Just then, the car stopped short, propelling them forward and causing their upper legs to connect. Jamie sucked in her breath at the contact. Immediately—and unfortunately—they pulled back, but not before she felt the pressure of Whit's knee against hers.

"Sorry," he said quickly.

"Don't be," she replied. *Touch me again*, she added silently.

When they arrived at the hotel, Whit insisted on walking her to her room. "What kind of gentleman would I be if I didn't?" he asked. Together they rode the elevator to the seventeenth floor. Despite standing on opposite sides, they continued to drink one another in. It was as if having visually locked in on each other, neither of them could let go.

"Thank you again for a great day," she said. "I still can't believe you rented out an entire spa for me."

"Totally worth it just to see your face."

Finally, something to force her gaze away. With her attention focused on the elevator railing, she told him, "I wish you wouldn't say things like that."

Every word he said intensified the feelings swirling inside her. And there were a lot of feelings.

"Even if it's true?"

That wasn't helping. It looked like she was in for another long night of lying alone in her bed, fantasizing about him. Somehow when Whit told her to keep on dreaming, she doubted that was what he meant.

Finally, the elevator doors slid open and they headed down the corridor. Jamie reached into her back pocket for the room key. All the while she felt Whit's eyes on her. He hadn't stopped watching her since the car ride began. The scrutiny sent an unwanted ache spooling between her legs.

"So," she said when they reached her door. "I'll see you tomorrow?"

"Tomorrow," he repeated. "Bright and early."

"Bright and early is good. I'll be there."

"I'll be waiting."

"I'm going to go in, then," she said.

"All right."

There was really nothing else to say except goodbye. So why couldn't she get out the word? She couldn't seem to do anything but stand there, her eyes locked on his.

"I—I should go," she stammered. She waited a moment to see if Whit would say something else. When he didn't, she turned and pressed the key card to the magnetic door lock. The latch clicked.

"Jamie?"

She whipped around before he'd even finished the second syllable. "Yes?"

His mouth dropped to her lips and back, turning her legs to jelly. "I'd really like to kiss you right now," he muttered.

Thank God.

She must have said the words out loud because suddenly, his hands were cradling her face and they were kissing with a day's worth of pent-up hunger. On and on they kissed, Whit's tongue sweeping inside her mouth as though he couldn't kiss her deep enough.

Her back against the door, Jamie slid her leg up and pressed the inside of her thigh against his hip. This was an absolutely horrible idea on so many, many levels, but she didn't care. She wanted it too much to stop.

"It's been killing me not to touch you," he groaned between kisses. "I've wanted to all day."

"I've wanted you to..." She didn't finish because he was kissing her again and she was thrusting her hips toward his. *Please*, she silently begged. *Please*.

When they broke apart, they were both gasping for breath. Whit's eyes were blown black. "May I come inside?" he asked.

Jamie handed him her key card.

CHAPTER EIGHT

THEY RETURNED TO kissing as soon as the door clicked shut behind them. "Are you sure about this?" Whit asked as he fumbled to blindly unbutton her coat.

"Yes," she replied between kisses. Yes, she was. Damn the risk. She had wanted his touch all day. Now that his hands were on her, there was no extinguishing the fire.

"Because..." He nibbled her lower lip. "I don't want to put you in an awkward... Ah..." His sentence ended on a throaty moan when she palmed him firmly through his jeans.

"I'm not asking for a lifetime commitment here, Whit. I'm just asking you to make love to me." Before she lost her mind. Her fingers reached for buttons only to have him lift her hands away. "I—"

"Hold on a minute." He brushed away her frown with his thumb. "Let me send the car home first. If I'm staying, I plan to take all night." His voice was imbued with husky promise.

While Whit sent away the driver, Jamie let her coat slide to the ground. Her sweater followed. By the time Whit hung up, she'd undone her zipper and stood waiting in her bra and gaping jeans.

Whit let out a rough-sounding obscenity that sent shivers up and down her spine. "No fair starting without me."

"I left you the good part."

"You certainly did." She watched as he peeled off layers of his own. Coat. Sweater. Belt. Each layer closing the gap between them until they stood toe to toe. Jamie let her eyes take in the glorious sight of his naked chest. He was more beautiful than she remembered. Lean and hard, with muscles honed from years of controlling a horse with his body. Her hands itched to cling to his broad shoulders.

She gasped as he pulled her against him. They were finally skin to skin. His eyes were hungry and heavy-lidded. "Now we're on the same page," he said and slanted his mouth over hers.

Jamie didn't think after that. She lost herself in the sensations building inside her. This wasn't two kids rolling around in a dorm room. This was two adults who knew how to give and receive intense pleasure. Their hands and mouths explored every inch of one another until they were both shaking with need. And when they finally tumbled over the edge, they tumbled together.

This wasn't how Whit had expected the day to end. He'd tried so hard to ignore his growing attraction to Jamie. Told himself it would be unprofessional—not to mention foolish—to revisit the past in that way. Reality seldom lived up to memories, wasn't that the rule? If that was the case, then the rule was wrong. The sex they'd just had blew him away. Dozens of nights in college—hell, dozens of nights with women, period—couldn't compare. Tonight was different from anything he'd ever experienced. It was intense. Explosive.

He nuzzled his nose into the crook of Jamie's neck. She lay spooned against him, in the same position he'd pulled her into when he'd returned to bed. "Sleeping?" he whispered.

"No. Thinking," she replied.

Thinking could be dangerous, especially if she regretted her decision to spend the night with him. Was she having second thoughts? "Good thoughts, I hope," he said before pressing a kiss to her shoulder.

"What do you think?"

That he couldn't tell from her voice, that's what he thought. "I think that I don't want to leave this bed for the next twenty-four hours."

"Only twenty-four?"

"Any longer and my heart might give out from the exertion. That was…" Struggling to find a word that didn't sound clichéd, he punctuated the sentence with another kiss instead.

Apparently, Jamie felt the same, since her reply was a sleepy, "Mmm…"

"No regrets then?"

She broke free of his embrace and rolled over to face him. There was hair in her face and her lips were swollen from kissing. "Do you really have to ask?"

The tips of his fingers traced the curve of her shoulder and down her arm. "Maybe I just want to make sure."

"I would think that was obvious by the way I screamed your name."

Whit smiled, remembering. Her cry had been what pushed him over the edge. "I don't mean the sex." He knew she was satisfied.

"I meant... Never mind." This wasn't the time to entertain doubts. Jamie was in his bed again, and he'd enjoy being with her for as long she would let him stay. *One day at a time*, to quote the sobriety literature.

In a way, being with Jamie was like being high. It came with the same cloud of euphoria except he wasn't alone. Eventually he'd come down—you always came down—but damn if he wouldn't try holding on to the sensation for as long as possible.

"To answer your question, yes. I am happy. This was the most amazing day."

The amount of relief her answer brought surprised him. Every muscle in his body relaxed. "Good," he whispered, his fingers slipping up and back down her spine. "That makes the day totally worthwhile."

A twinkle appeared in her eyes, bright even in the low light. "Day's not over yet. We've still got a few hours left."

Whit laughed. "Oh, my God, what do you think I am, a machine?" Even as he said it, however, he felt himself stirring. The things this woman was doing to him today.

"Well, if you're not..."

She started to roll over, but he caught her by the midsection. "Whoa, whoa, whoa. What do you think you're doing?" he asked.

"Going to sleep?"

"Not yet. Like you said, there's still time left in the day."

Pushing aside his own disconcerting thoughts, he rolled on top of her and proceeded to make the most of it.

The next morning Jamie awoke to the smell of fresh coffee. "Sleeping Beauty awakes," Whit greeted her when she lifted her head. He set a coffee mug on the nightstand. "I was afraid I'd have to kiss you awake, and God knows where that would have ended up." Despite his joke, he leaned over and kissed her. He tasted like mint and coffee. "Morning," he whispered.

"What are you doing up?" Squinting at the

clock on her nightstand, Jamie saw it was barely six thirty. She turned her attention back to him and saw he wore his gray V-neck sweater. "Why are you dressed?"

"Workday. Thought it would be a good idea if I went to my apartment and changed before heading into the office. Wouldn't want people thinking I'd spent the night rolling around a hotel bed. Even if I did. How are you this morning?"

"Tired," she said. "In a good way though."

"I know what you mean," he said, brushing some errant strands of hair from her face.

"My hair must be a mess." She could feel what was left of her bun hanging loosely by her ear. Then again, what did she expect after last night? That's what happened when you were determined to make the hours count.

Whit smiled and smoothed back another lock of hair. "You look sexed up. It's a good look on you. I ordered you breakfast. Fruit and croissants. They're in the other room."

"You're not going to stay?"

"Can't. I've got some business to take care of before we meet."

Jamie wasn't sure what one had to do with the other, but she wasn't going to let her disappointment show. She was a big girl and knew going into this that last night wasn't about anything other than scratching an itch, so she reverted to what she used to do in college and feigned indifference. Using her pillow as a distraction, she made a show of fluffing it so she could push herself into a sitting position. "Okay. I'll see you at the office then," she said casually without looking up.

"Sounds good." She'd moved to fussing with the covers in her lap when Whit caught her chin and lifted her face to his. Without their sexual glaze, his eyes were once again clear and blue, but strangely unreadable. They roamed over her features like they were searching for something—what, she couldn't guess—before softening. He kissed her sweetly, ending the moment with a swipe of his thumb over her bottom lip. "See you soon," he said.

After he left, Jamie stayed in bed, drinking her coffee and reliving the night. She thought about calling Keisha, but her friend would be getting ready for work. More importantly, Jamie wasn't in the mood for a lecture on how sleeping with Whit was a gateway to trouble. This wasn't college with her secretly yearning for Whit to be her Prince Charming. She went into last night with no expectations, emotional or otherwise.

Good thing too, because not even in her wildest dreams could she have imagined how last night would turn out. Jamie was no stranger to good sex, but this... She must have died a thousand little deaths. She could still feel him between her legs.

Regardless, she knew better than to build the night into anything lasting. She'd let this affair, this one-night stand, this however-long-it-lasted thing, run its course and then say goodbye afterwards. No broken heart. No wishing for more.

And if she believed all that, she might as well believe unicorns were real too.

Whit was behind closed doors on the phone when Jamie arrived at his office. Whoever the caller was, they were having a heated conversation; Whit's voice could be heard through the door. "I was looking for support. You're the one who decided to call the handlers."

Handlers? A few feet away, several employees smiled awkwardly at her from their cubicles. "Has he been on the phone long?" she asked one of them.

"Don't know. They were talking when I came in," he answered.

Maybe she'd go to the breakroom and pour herself a cup of coffee she didn't want. Curious as she was, she didn't want to get caught eavesdropping. She was turning around when Whit's voice sounded again. "Go ahead, cut me out. It's not going to stop me from telling my story."

Wait, they were talking about the book?

"I don't care what you think," Whit said. "If I'm going to carry this shame around for the rest of my life, I'm going to damn well make it count for something!" There was a slamming sound and a few seconds later the door flew open. Whit stood in the opening, his jaw clenching in anger. Behind his glasses, his eyes glittered with anger.

Jamie gave an awkward smile before showing him the paper sack she was holding. "I brought you a croissant."

When he saw her, embarrassment crept into his face. "Tell me you didn't hear any of that conversation," he said.

"Okay. I didn't hear any of that conversation," she replied before pointing to the cubicles and adding, "Neither did any of them."

He let out a long breath. "Come on in."

"Are you okay?" she asked as he let her pass. "Do you want to get some coffee or head up to the roof?"

"Thanks, but I'm fine." He pointed to the large paper cup on his desk in what she presumed was an answer to both offers. "Do you?"

"I had my fill at the hotel. Who was on the phone?" Whoever had called, they weren't happy about the book, that much was clear. "Was that your father?"

"Grandfather. Apparently, he got my message about the book."

"You mean he didn't already know? I thought you said they were okay with you writing your story." In fact, she could have sworn they'd discussed this very point over lunch on the first day.

"Actually, I believe I said I'd handle my family. Technically, I don't need their permission or approval to do anything."

"You hadn't told him yet?"

"He was in the Far East," Whit replied before returning to his desk chair. "I left him a message to let me know when he returned, and I would call him. He got back yesterday." Jamie set her materials on the conference table. Talking to his grandfather must have been the "business" Whit had mentioned this morning.

"Sounds like he was giving you a hard time. I'm sorry." And here she'd thought Whit's grandfather might have respected him for taking control of his life. Hadn't she been mistaken. She wondered if Whit ever got any emotional support from his family.

"Did I hear correctly that he was threatening to fire you from the foundation?"

"Not fire me. Disown me."

Her jaw dropped. "You're kidding." Over a personal memoir? Was the family reputation that important to the man?

The last thing she wanted was for Whit to lose

everything because of a stupid book. "Look, if that's the case, maybe we should stop…"

"Absolutely not," Whit replied firmly. "This is my story, not his. He's already robbed me of closure once. I'm not going to let him bully me into staying silent completely."

What did he mean, robbed him of closure? "But your inheritance. The foundation. Can he really take that away from you when you set it up?" she argued.

He spun a pen he'd picked up from his desk. "Technically, yes, because it's a family foundation spending Martin money. I don't care; let him take his money and his name. I can form another foundation by myself."

Regardless of his bravado, his grandfather's ultimatum hurt. Jamie could see the pain lurking behind the anger. And it wasn't just the threat of losing the foundation that he'd invested so much time and energy in. It was the confirmation that his grandfather had chosen the family reputation over his grandson.

"I'm still sorry," she said. "For what it's worth, I think what you're doing is pretty impressive."

He barked out a laugh.

"What's so funny?" she asked.

"Saying that telling the world I used to be strung out on drugs and drink is impressive."

"It is." She didn't know why he couldn't see

the beauty in what he was doing. "You're standing in your truth."

"More wisdom from your previous subject?"

"No, this one is pure Jamie Rutkowski."

"Well, in that case…" Their eyes met, and he looked at her with a tenderness so sweet it made her heart cry.

He blinked and the moment disappeared. "May I have my croissant?" he asked.

The abruptness of the shift left her off balance, and she had to think before remembering the pastry. The paper bag from the hotel sat on the table behind her. "It's raspberry," she said, handing him the sack. "I ate the chocolate ones. Good morning, by the way."

"Good morning to you too, Ms. Rutkowski," he replied, his overly formal greeting marred by a mischievous smile. "May I say that your hair's looking much neater than the last time I saw you."

"Thank you. Turns out hair's much easier to style when someone doesn't have his hands tangled in it."

"Touché." He tore off the corner of the pastry and popped it into his mouth. "Is that your way of suggesting I should keep my hands to myself?"

"Not really, but since you brought up the subject, it's not a bad idea," she said, ignoring her own urge to lick the crumbs off his lower lip.

"Spoilsport."

"Hey, if you want to continue ticking off your grandfather, we're going to have to get this book drafted. We still have a lot of ground to cover."

"My oh-so-impressive truth that I'm standing in."

"Precisely," she said, choosing to ignore the skepticism that had leaked back into his voice.

While Whit finished his pastry, she got out her equipment. First, she positioned the voice recorder on his desk to make sure they got a decent recording. Then she grabbed her pen and notebook. "The other day you told me about taking painkillers after your injury. The prescription was only for…" She flipped a few pages. "Seven days. Then you borrowed from teammates. How did that work?"

"Easy. I went up and asked if they had any extra pills they weren't using. There are plenty of professional players who save their leftover pain pills after an injury. You never know when you might tweak something."

"But if you were hitting them up all the time, wouldn't they eventually run out themselves?"

"They did. That's when I started going to dealers."

He proceeded to tell her about how, after a few close calls buying off the street, he'd discovered there was a black market on the internet where people could buy any kind of drug they wanted, as long as they had the money. "And I had the money," he told her simply. Jamie listened while he talked about needing higher and higher dosages to manage the pain. "And, if I didn't have enough, there was always alcohol. Lots and lots of alcohol," he said.

The self-abuse got so bad that eventually the team cut him for failing a drug test. From there on his life became a never-ending cycle of painkillers and booze.

"Oh, and partying. Don't forget that," he said dryly. "So long as you're in a crowd having a good time, you pretend your life isn't falling apart around you."

Alone in a crowded room. Sounded familiar. Whit was watching her scribble down notes. "Are you impressed yet?" he asked sarcastically.

She was impressed he was alive and healthy today. Rather than say anything, however, Jamie flipped over a page on her notebook. He was goading her on purpose. Until today, he'd been reluctant—painfully so—to tell her the darker parts of his story. Today he was doing his best to emphasize them.

"I know what you're doing," she said. He'd taken her comments about standing in his truth as a challenge and was doing his best to prove her wrong. "You're trying to horrify me. It won't work."

What Whit didn't realize was that telling her the worst of the worst had the opposite effect on her than he'd probably imagined. The lower his fall got and the more sordid his stories became, the more impressive he became in her eyes. When demons had such a strong hold on you, it took way more than money to claw your way back. You needed real strength of character.

"Who were you partying with at this point?" she asked, since his teammates were no longer in the picture.

"You can always find someone who will party with you if you've got enough money. Other times I picked up someone in one of the nightclubs and took her—or them—home."

No surprise there. Jamie gripped her pen a little tighter. Of course, he'd had partners between college and last night; she had too. That didn't stop her from feeling jealous of all of them.

Moving on before he could say any more, she asked, "Didn't your family notice all the money you were spending?" From the stories, it sounded as though he was going through money hand over fist.

"My grandfather called a few times after he saw photos of me in the press. That one with the models and the champagne bottles really set him off."

"Go figure," Jamie said dryly.

"But as far as the money went, I doubt they noticed. Even if they did, there wasn't a lot they could do. I inherited an enormous trust fund when I turned twenty-three, so the money was mine to spend."

She couldn't believe no one in his family had noticed. Didn't they call and talk to him? Visit him? Even her parents, busy as they were, managed to call once in a while. She shouldn't be surprised though. Not really. Whit's parents didn't seem to notice a lot of things where he was concerned.

So many of Whit's stories had a disturbing commonality to them. Whit was alone. Other than his cousin, Monty, he hadn't mentioned another close friend. The people he mentioned were teammates or acquaintances. And those friends who were close to him, like Terrance, had no idea about Whit's past. If they did, Keisha would have heard and subsequently so would she.

Basically, Whit had been in Europe drowning with no one close enough to care about him. For that matter, how many people were ever close enough to him to care?

Besides her.

"Okay," she said as she swallowed hard to clear away the frog in her throat. "You've got unlimited funds which means you never have to worry about being homeless or needing money for drugs and booze. How do you hit rock bottom?"

Until now Whit had been feigning nonchalance by rocking back and forth in his desk chair, but when Jamie asked her question, he stopped rocking. "Hard," he replied.

That much was obvious. "How so? Was it a gradual wakeup call or," as she strongly suspected, "did something happen to cause it?"

Instead of answering, Whit reached for his coffee. It must have grown cold ages ago, but he took a long drink anyway. Buying time while he worked out where to start, probably. She remembered Frankie Johnson doing the same thing during the more painful parts of his interview. She gave Whit the same advice she'd given him. "Sometimes it works best to go straight to the bottom line. Then we can go back and fill in the details."

He nodded and clenched his jaw, giving his face a hardened cast. "Bottom line, huh?"

"Uh-huh. Don't worry about sugarcoating it or anything like that. Just spit out the words."

"All right. The day I hit rock bottom…"

He took a deep breath. Jamie didn't realize at first, but she'd taken one too. She held it waiting for the answer.

"Was the day I let a woman die."

His voice choked on the words. But they were out. For the first time he'd admitted the truth out loud. The shameful, horrible truth. He, Whitmore Martin, heir to the Martin fortune—for now—and former opioid-addicted reprobate, had let a woman die. Having finally let his secret free, he waited for the closure he was supposed to feel. There was no sense of closure. Only the same nauseating shame that always churned in his stomach.

He watched while Jamie tried to hide her shock. No surprise that she couldn't do it. Who could upon hearing the man they'd just slept with had blood on his hands?

"I don't understand," she said slowly. "What do you mean?"

She wasn't alone. There were days when he couldn't understand how it had happened either. Giving a sigh, he tossed his glasses onto the desk. Talking would be easier if he couldn't read Jamie's eyes. "You've seen photos of the Isle of Capri, haven't you?"

"The island off of Italy? Not really, but I know the place."

"It's gorgeous. Little multicolored fish, turquoise waters and giant rock formations. You can only get there by helicopter or boat."

He paused to see if she would say anything. She didn't.

"I was staying on the Amalfi Coast, crashing at the villa of a guy I'd met in Salerno. Ricardo something. He was a jerk, but he threw good parties. By this time, I was living in a haze anyway. Partying all night, sleeping all day. If I did drag my ass out of bed before sunset, I started drinking as soon as I could. Being wasted was the only way I could avoid thinking about what a total loser I'd become."

"And no one in the house noticed?"

"Are you kidding? They were all as bad as me." Why did she keep asking him that question? Hadn't she figured out by now that no one cared about him? He only mattered for what he could do for them. Provide an heir, preserve a legacy, keep the party going with drink and drugs. If he'd dropped dead on a nightclub floor, his entourage would have been more concerned about how they would have paid the bar tab.

"Anyway, one day," he continued, "Ricardo heard that some friends of a friend were throwing a party on his yacht. A lot of models, aspiring models, pretend models. That sort of thing. They were going to head to Capri so the girls could swim in the grottos and invited us to go along." He remembered Ricardo jumping at the invitation. "They always have the hottest women, Ricardo told me. It will blow your mind."

Jamie's pen tapped against her notepad, impatient for him to finish and explain what he'd meant before. She wouldn't have long to wait.

Whit pushed himself to his feet. The space behind his desk had suddenly become too close and confining. He needed to move. After crossing the room, he pressed his palms to the glass block wall. Behind him, he heard Jamie's chair squeak as she turned around.

"The party was amazing. We anchored offshore, by the White Grotto, and spent the day drinking and swimming. The guy who owned the yacht—do you know I still don't know his name? Ricardo was right, he knew some gorgeous women. And the wine… Man, it was flowing like water. We kept it up for eighteen, nineteen hours straight."

"Sounds insane."

"It was, and I'd been to some wild parties. Anyway, there was this one girl. Bianca DeLuca." A name he would never forget.

"She was hard-core. It was about two in the morning and she and I were stretched out on the bow chairs, having one of those philosophical discussions that only make sense when you're totally drunk. We'd found a stash of Cristal and had stolen a couple bottles. 'One for each of us,' she'd joked."

"You did this after eighteen hours of drinking in the sun?"

"Told you it was insane," Whit replied. *Stupid* would be a better word. "She dared me to keep up with her, so I was matching her drink for drink. It was a bad idea. I ended up hurling over the side into the sea. Super classy." And the least of his crimes, as it turned out.

"I was sick for quite a while and by the time I'd finished, Bianca had passed out. I poked her a few times trying to wake her up, but she wouldn't budge. Finally, I said 'suit yourself' and passed out myself. When I woke up a few hours later, she was dead."

CHAPTER NINE

Now that he'd told the story, shame cut through him like a knife, forcing him to squeeze his eyes shut. In his mind, the memory played out in excruciating detail. Bianca's cold skin, her pale parted lips. "At first, I thought she was still asleep, but then I saw her face and I knew. It turned out she'd been popping pills all day. She must have taken some more while we were drinking."

"Whit…" There was the sound of footsteps and Jamie was suddenly behind him. Her hand on his shoulder.

"I killed her," he whispered. "I walked away from her and left her to die."

Jamie couldn't stand listening to the pain in his voice. Wrapping her arms around his shoulders, she hugged him as tightly as she could.

"Don't," he said, pulling free. "I don't deserve any sympathy."

He didn't deserve the blame either, at least not to the level he was punishing himself. "What happened wasn't your fault," she said.

"Weren't you listening to me?" He slapped the glass before turning around and glaring at her.

"It's all my fault. A woman is dead because I was too messed up to do anything to help her!"

The office outside his door went silent.

"Terrific," Whit said harshly. "So much for controlling the message." Brushing past her, he returned to his desk to put on his glasses. "The other day at lunch, you asked me why I wanted to write this book," he said, keeping his back to her. "Now you know. Maybe I can stop some other poor schmuck from letting someone else die."

Jamie watched as his shoulders rose and fell. So much pain and anger whirling inside him and so little forgiveness. How could she make him see that it was all right to forgive himself?

They couldn't continue the discussion here, that was certain. The walls were too thin.

"Come on," she told him. After gathering up her belongings, she shoved them back in her bag, then took his hand. "We're getting out of here."

"Jamie, I…"

He sounded spent. "We're going someplace private," she told him. "I've got things I want to say to you and there are too many ears around here. So come on, let's get our coats."

Taking his hand, she tugged until he gave in and started moving. As soon as they opened the door, however, he took the lead, walking down the corridor with his head held high and his shoulders straight, as though he hadn't said a self-condemning word. It wasn't easy. Jamie could tell from the tension in his jaw that it took a lot of energy to behave with such nonchalance.

"Down," she said when they reached the elevator. While she'd considered going up to the rooftop, there was no guarantee someone else from the building might not also decide to get fresh air, and this was a discussion that demanded total privacy. That's why she was taking him back to the hotel.

Thankfully, the maid had already come and gone, meaning there would be no interruptions. Jamie hung the Do Not Disturb sign on the door handle and shut the door. When she turned around, she found Whit standing in the center of the living area with his overcoat still on. Other than telling her there was nothing she could say, he'd stayed quiet during the five-block walk. Tossing her own coat on the sofa, Jamie headed to the corner that doubled as the suite's bar and coffee station. "Do you want something? Coffee? Water?" she asked before cracking the lid off one of the bottled waters.

"Was it really necessary to come all the way back here?" Whit asked.

"Yes, it was. There's no need for your office, or anyone else, to hear our conversation." A bit ironic since the conversation would eventually be very public. "Like you said yourself, control the message."

"Fine," he said following a resigned sigh. Still wearing his overcoat, he settled onto one of the bar stools. "We'll talk. Not that there's anything for you to say."

"Oh, I've got plenty to say," Jamie shot back. "And you're going to listen. What happened on that yacht was tragic. It should never have happened. But…" She cut him off before he could say anything. "It was an accident. A horribly tragic accident."

"Which could have been prevented if I'd done something to help her."

"What could you have done?"

"I could have tried harder to wake her up," he said. "I could have called for help. Woken up someone so we could take her to shore, to a hospital. I could have done *something*." He pounded his fist on the marble counter, hard enough that Jamie feared he might hurt himself. If he did, he'd probably take the pain as a just punishment. "But I didn't. I just crawled off and fell asleep."

"You passed out," she corrected him. "You were drunk."

"It doesn't matter. I still should have done something." His head dropped to his hands. "If I'd been sober, none of this would have happened."

"If you'd been sober, Whit, you wouldn't have been on the yacht in the first place." It was Jamie's turn to slap the counter. She slammed her bottle hard down enough to send water shooting from the neck.

"Tell me something," she said. "Where did Bianca get the pills? Did you give them to her?"

"No. She had them in her bag. They found the empty bottle in with her towel."

"Did you see her take them?'"

He shook his head. "Too busy getting drunk."

"In other words, you didn't give her the pills and you didn't watch her take the pills. Do you see where I'm going here? If you didn't know she was taking the pills, how could you possibly know that she'd overdosed?"

She could tell by Whit's expression that he was going to try fighting her logic. Jamie bit back her frustration. There was no need for him to torture himself like this.

She walked around the bar and stood in front of him. Grasping his face with both hands, she forced him to look her in the eye. "Listen to me. What happened to that woman was an accident. She was the one who brought the pills on board. She's the one who chose to take them. You are *not* responsible for her choices."

"I'm responsible for mine, though," he whispered.

"But you didn't do anything."

"Exactly. I didn't." He placed his hands over hers. Jamie waited for him to lift them away, but he didn't. Instead, he leaned forward to rest his forehead against hers. His eyes closed. "The last thing I said to her was, 'I hope you choke on that champagne.' She'd laughed when I threw up the first time and I said, 'I hope you choke…'"

Oh, Whit. Was that why he was punishing himself? For words he hadn't really meant? "It still doesn't make her death your fault. You didn't know she was going to die."

Now he lifted her hands, and, kissing the flesh of her palm, set them on his lap. "I know what you're trying to do," he said. "The therapists at the rehab center told me the same things. None of you understand. I may not be directly responsible for her death, but I was there. You say she made a choice? Well, I made a choice too. Lots of them. And because of my choices, a woman died who might not have if I'd acted differently. No matter what I do, I'm going to bear that responsibility for the rest of my life."

All of a sudden, pieces began falling in place. "She's the reason you went to rehab," Jamie said. "And why you started the foundation."

"I thought if I could do enough good, I might make up for all the mistakes I'd made." He looked at her with a haunted expression, the pain in his eyes tearing her insides in two. "I've made so many wrong choices, Jams."

"We all have, Whit."

"Not like this," he said, standing up and walking to the center of the room before Jamie could reach out to him. Hands stuffed in his overcoat, he stood staring at the artwork that hung above the sofa. The image was a black-and-white photograph of the carousel in Central Park.

What she wouldn't give to be back in Central Park laughing the way they'd done yesterday. Things had flipped one hundred eighty degrees in only a few hours.

"When we finally got back to the continent, I made the mistake of calling my family," Whit said heavily. "I thought they deserved a heads-up in case anything became public."

"Was that the only reason?" Jamie asked.

"You mean was it a cry for help? I suppose it was. I was a mess; I can tell you that much. Standing in a piazza, hungover and stinking of stale champagne. Next thing I know, my grandfather's hired handlers were hustling me on a plane to Switzerland. They also managed to make the whole incident disappear."

"What?"

"The scandal can't hit the media if it doesn't exist. It's what my family does. Told you, the family legacy is everything."

Jamie tried to wrap her head around what Whit was saying. How could you make an overdose victim disappear? They must have paid off everyone involved. "What about Bianca's family?" she asked. "Surely they'd want to know how their daughter died."

"I'm sure they were told a plausible story and compensated for their grief."

"That's terrible," she said. On so many levels. Including for Whit, who couldn't openly acknowledge his guilt and grief. No wonder he wanted to write this book. He was shining a light on the truth. This was his apology to Bianca.

"Hardly the man you knew in college, is it?" he said bitterly.

"No, you're not." This Whit was flawed and broken. He was also strong and giving.

"You must think I'm awful."

"On the contrary. I think you're amazing." His mouth parted in surprise. "For you to be standing here after everything that happened, and still be the strong, kind, gentle man you are…? It's incredible."

"But Bianca…"

"Was a horrible accident," she repeated. "But that doesn't make you a monster. Not to me."

Seizing the lapels of his overcoat, she pulled him close. "Not to me," she repeated, kissing him. "Not to me." Over and over, she repeated the words while showering him with kisses, hoping he would come to believe her. She wrestled him out of his overcoat and loosened the collar on his shirt. "Not to me," she whispered against his Adam's apple.

A tortured-sounding groan rose from Whit as he suddenly pulled her tight. Jamie found herself in a maelstrom she was happy to ride out. She moaned in response as Whit's mouth devoured hers, finesse shoved aside in favor of raw need. He tugged impatiently at the belt on her wrap dress. "Need you," he said as the material parted. It was close to a plea. "Need you so much."

"Then take me," Jamie replied simply. The mixture of gratitude and desire that appeared in his eyes stole her breath.

He slipped the dress off her shoulders and dropped to his knees.

Later, when they'd caught their breath and made it to the bedroom, Jamie lay with her head on Whit's chest. Her fingers played lazily with the soft sandy hairs on his chest.

"Mmm…feels nice," he said. His fingers skimmed the sensitive skin on her back in return. "Why did I not appreciate you more in college?"

"Because you were stupid?"

His laugh vibrated against her ear. "That must be it. Total stupidity. Thank you," he added in a softer voice.

"You don't have to thank me for saying the truth."

"I want to. I have been living with that story

trapped inside me for almost two years. I was desperate to tell someone, but at the same time… I thought you'd be totally disgusted when you heard it."

"You could never disgust me," she told him. *I love you too much.*

"What's wrong? You just got tense."

"Sorry. Muscle twitch." Taking deep breaths, she consciously slowed her heart rate. "I'm better now."

The mattress dipped as he raised his head. "You sure?" he asked. "I can massage it if you want."

"There's nothing to massage. I am completely boneless and muscle-less at this point."

Which was why she couldn't be in love with Whit, but rather reacting to an emotionally intense afternoon. To think she'd gone and fallen over the edge would be as foolish as thinking Whit's "need" for her meant anything beyond a desire to banish his dark thoughts.

"Do you feel better now?" she asked, getting back to the topic at hand.

"Mmm… I do feel lighter. I'll always carry the guilt of 'what if' or wishing I'd acted differently. But I feel better at the thought of making it public."

"I can't believe your grandfather swept the entire incident under the rug."

"No scandals, no black marks on the sainted

Martin legacy, barring a few robber barons, that is, but they kept their vices private so it's okay." There was humor in his voice, but Jamie bet if she lifted her head, it would be missing from his eyes.

A thought occurred to her. "Your cousin Monty's car accident. Was he...?"

"The one who crossed the yellow line and not the other driver? I can't prove it, but yeah, I think so. It's a little too ironic otherwise. Especially considering Monty had a few DUIs erased in the past."

One more secret he was unable to share. Jamie kissed his chest, earning a sleepy-sounding sigh.

"S'funny," he continued. "I've never told anyone my suspicions about Monty. Seems like I'm always telling you things."

"I'd take that as a compliment if you weren't supposed to be telling me things," she replied.

"Not for the book, silly. In general. I don't... That is, I'm not the kind of person who shares a lot. Not even with my closest friends like Terrance. But you? You're different than the others. I can talk to you. Always could." The last part was said in the middle of a yawn.

"You have a different memory of college than I do," she said as she struggled against making more of the compliment than there probably was. "I shared and we did talk sometimes. You were just way more interested in making out."

He chuckled. "We've already established that I was stupid."

"And horny."

"That too. What can I say? It was my shallow period." He yawned again and when he started speaking, his words were slow and sleepy. "But if I was going to talk more back then, it would have been with you. I really was stupid, wasn't I?"

"Yes, you were." Jamie nearly choked on the lump in her throat. Damn him for implying she was special and making her all emotional.

Lifting her head, she saw that Whit's eyes had closed. The tension was gone from his features, making him look younger and at peace. He was still the most handsome man she knew. Her heart swooped at the sight.

She was on the precipice again. *Back up*, the voice in her head warned. *Don't let your heart fall over the edge.*

Her heart really didn't want to listen. Her heart looked at the man lying next to her and saw someone who didn't recognize his own strength and sensitivity. Like those Japanese bowls whose cracks were filled with gold, Whit was better for his flaws.

Was it possible, she wondered, that those cracks had been there all along? Had she, blinded by his golden boy status, simply failed to notice them? She felt like, for the first time, she was truly seeing Whit for the man he was. Every conversation with him revealed yet another layer.

What was she going to do this summer, when Keisha's wedding had passed, and Whit's memoir was written? Did she really think their affair would continue without an excuse to see each other? No matter how hard Jamie tried to think otherwise, she couldn't shake the fear that she was nothing more than a familiar presence at a time when Whit badly needed someone to support him.

But what if this time was different from when they were in college? What if this time, Whit recognized how much she loved him and let himself love her back? Her heart pushed against the resolve she'd wrapped around it, whispering little words of hope and encouragement.

And what if this wasn't any different? her head insisted. What if history simply repeated itself? What would she do then? No, she decided. Better to keep her resolve and save her heart from crumbling.

A barely visible hint of five o'clock shadow was starting on Whit's cheek. As she brushed the back of her hand against the slightly rough surface, Jamie swallowed the tightness in her throat.

Along with the fear that her heart wasn't going to listen to a word her head was saying.

CHAPTER TEN

Three months later

"YOU'RE MAKING THE bed shake."

"Sorry."

The shaking stopped, only to resume a few moments later. Trying not to smile, Whit reached over and laid his right hand on Jamie's thigh.

"Sorry," she repeated. "I get fidgety."

"No kidding. Maybe I should take this in the other room."

"No, don't." Her hand was on his before he could pull the sheet back. "I'll stop fidgeting."

To prove it, she tucked both legs beneath her. When she did, the top edge of the sheet dropped to her ribcage, creating an entirely different kind of distraction.

What on earth made him think he could read in bed?

They were in Jamie's apartment, spending a warm spring afternoon tangled in crisp cotton sheets. The purpose of the visit was to read the penultimate chapters of his memoir. They'd both agreed that Bianca's story be written last as those chapters would be the most difficult, both to draft and to read. As soon as Jamie had called to tell him they were finished, he'd flown to Boston to read them.

Somehow the notion of email managed to escape them both. Whit leaped at the chance to see her, just as he'd leaped at every other excuse he could invent over the past three months.

He wasn't used to someone taking up so much space in his mind the way she did. The way she listened to him, the way she made him feel better about himself, it was addictive and that frightened him. In his experience, addictions always ended badly. But denial being a man's best friend, he'd ignored the fear in favor of another taste of her.

His hello kiss had lasted seventy-five minutes.

It was only after, when he was able to concentrate on other business, that she'd handed him her laptop with the pages queued up.

She had been bouncing her leg up and down ever since.

"I don't know why you're so nervous," he told her. "I loved everything else you wrote. There's no reason to think I won't love this too."

"The other stuff wasn't nearly as emotional," she said. "This was a tragic and transformative moment in your life. It's important I get it right."

From what he'd read so far, she'd accomplished her mission. Whit was surprised at how disassociated he felt from the events on the page. Lying here, with Jamie's scent on his skin, those days in Italy seemed far away now. How different he felt from the lonely, pathetic addict on the page. Jamie had managed to capture every ounce of his pain and desolation, making him sympathetic without minimizing the depravity of his actions.

She was good at that, making him seem better than he was.

I can't count the times I've wished time would roll back to that night. Would it have changed the outcome? I don't know, but I could have tried. She would at least have died knowing someone cared about her life. I can only hope she knows she made a difference in mine.

Wow. Blinking back the dampness, he turned away from the page to look at Jamie, who had switched to gnawing her lip.

"Okay?" she asked.

"More than okay. It's great." Her face lit up, making him light up too. "Have you sent the pages to Amanda?" Amanda was Jamie's, and now his, literary agent. The early chapters had so blown her away that she'd offered to shop the book around to all her publishing contacts.

"Not yet," Jamie said. "I didn't want to do that until you'd had a chance to review them and make notes. When we have an absolute final draft, I'll send her the entire manuscript."

"Unbelievable." Despite having gone through it, the process still amazed him. "A few months ago, this was only a vague idea thought up during the engagement party and now, here it is, an entire book. One that's better than anything I could have written myself."

"You're only saying that because you're sleeping with the author."

"Yes, and because it's great. This," he said, tapping the top of the screen, "is exactly the story I wanted to tell. It doesn't pull any punches in terms of the truth."

The document, he noticed, had a different name than the other files he'd read. "*Falling.* Is that what you were thinking of for the title?"

"Maybe. Amanda and I brainstormed some ideas. We came up with *Fall: The Crash and Burn of an American Golden Boy.*"

"*Crash and Burn,*" Whit repeated thoughtfully. "Certainly apropos."

"Amanda thinks it'll grab readers' attention. I wanted to add something about the triumph of strength over darkness, but she thought it gave off the wrong vibe."

When she talked matter-of-factly like that, as if his worthiness was a foregone conclusion, Whit was overcome with humility. His chest felt stuffed to the point where he thought he might actually burst open.

At moments like this, he didn't trust his voice not to crack, so he settled for kissing her temple before turning back to the screen.

The conversation reminded him. "Since we're talking about titles, there's something I meant to bring up earlier."

"What?"

There needed to be a rule against naked women playing peek-a-boo with bedsheets. The view wreaked havoc on his concentration. Whit had to reach down and cover her up before he could speak. "Your name should go on the cover," he said.

"It can't. The book is your story."

"But you wrote it. Your words are what's bringing the pages to life." He'd been thinking about this for a while. All he'd done was answer questions while she'd spent hours organizing the information into a compelling narrative. Not to mention the hours she'd spent keeping him from falling apart. "You deserve to have everyone know you wrote this story."

She shook her head. "You don't understand. It's your story. I wrote it in the first person. From the mouth of America's Golden Boy himself."

"Then we'll use both names." He wasn't going to let this issue go. "This book wouldn't exist without you. I want people to know how important you were to me." There was more to his wish than highlighting her contribution though. If the book was a reminder of how low he'd fallen, it was also a reminder of how high she could go. A touchstone for her dreams.

There was a distant expression in Jamie's eyes when he looked at her. What looked like frown lines had appeared at the corners of her mouth.

"What's wrong? Don't you like the idea?"

"No, I... What you said about being important to you. Thank you."

Something in her voice sounded off, but he couldn't figure out what. Maybe she'd been caught off-guard, or, knowing her, doubted it was true. "I meant every word."

The lines disappeared into a smile. "Thank you." She leaned in and kissed him.

Whit turned to deepen the kiss. No sooner did his hand curl around her neck than he remembered the laptop, which was currently sliding off his hip toward the floor. Letting out a loud curse, he quickly turned in the opposite direction in time to catch the computer as it tumbled over the edge.

"Talk about a close call," he said. "Maybe I should turn this baby off before I cause any damage."

He was about to power it down when he noticed one of the drop-down menus had been expanded. In catching the computer, his hand must have clicked the mouse pad, opening a list of recently used documents. Second from the top was a document called Novel.

"Is this what I think it is?" He angled the screen so Jamie could see and got a bright pink blush in response.

"It's just an idea I've been playing around with," she said. "I've got a few chapters written and a bit of an outline. All very rough still."

Rough or not, she was writing her own material again. The knowledge made him very happy. "Will you let me read it when you finish?" he asked.

"If I finish. Like I said, it's only a few short chapters." While she had been speaking, she'd taken control of the laptop and closed the windows.

"Well, I have faith that you will. And that the finished product is going to be great."

"We'll see," she replied, snapping the computer closed. "Just because you chase a dream doesn't mean it comes true."

"And sometimes it does," he said before taking the laptop from her hands. Once he set the computer aside, he cupped her chin. "You're going after what you want, Jams. Have faith that you might get it." He gave her a long kiss, hoping she understood how much he wanted her to succeed. As usual, he needed only to touch her lips for his arousal to stir.

Definitely an addiction.

"Want to know what I'm dreaming about?" he whispered.

Her hands locked around his neck. "What?"

He showed her.

A few days later, Jamie sat in a hairdresser's chair, watching Keisha do a trial run of her wedding makeup. She told her about Whit adding her to the cover of the book as cowriter.

"I agree with him. After all that flying back and forth that you did, you deserve equal recognition. We're going to have to throw a book signing party so you can give us all signed copies."

"We have to sell the book first," Jamie replied.

"Girl, you and I both know that book will sell soon as they hear Whit's last name. People love dirt on rich families."

"My agent basically said the same thing. She wouldn't be surprised if publishers got into a bidding war over rights."

"Really? I take it all back then. You can throw the book signing party."

"Equal billing doesn't mean equal pay," Jamie told her. "I've already been paid for my work. Any money from the publisher goes to Whit, who plans to use it to fund more substance abuse programs."

Keisha closed her eyes so the makeup artist could dust her lids with gold metallic shadow. "Is that why you don't sound excited? Because of the money?"

"Not at all. I'm happy for the charities who will be getting the money," Jamie said. And she was proud of her work. Whit's memoir was some of the best writing she'd done yet. Her agent had predicted good things for her career.

"Then what's got you so bummed out?" Her friend turned her head and batted her eyes. "Do you think this is too much eye shadow?"

"You want it a little heavier for photographs. I'm not bummed out, by the way, I'm subdued. You know how I get after being submersed in a subject for a long time. Takes me a few days to decompress."

Possibly more in this case. Much harder to shake a subject when you were sleeping with him.

If she had to shake him. Jamie's mind hadn't decided which way that particular wind was blowing yet. One minute she'd tell herself not to get her hopes up. The next she'd see his eyes looking down at her with this mixture of tenderness and awe and her hopes would shoot skyward again.

Keisha stopped the makeup artist so she could

give Jamie the side eye. "Don't pull that decompress stuff with me. Something's bothering you. What is it? You're not sad about the wedding, are you? 'Cause you know the two of us are sisters for life."

"Damn straight," Jamie replied with a smile. "I'm planning of giving you a big, teary hug on your wedding day."

"Same here. Can you make sure that eyeliner is waterproof?" Keisha asked the makeup artist before doubling back to her original question. "If it's not the 'my best friend is getting married' blues, then what does have you down? Never mind. I already know. Whit," she sighed. "I knew it. Didn't I warn you?"

"We've been spending a lot of time together the past three months. The interviews got very intense and emotional. I mean, we weren't talking about model railroads." She looked down at her chair. There was a tear in the chair arm's plastic overlay, and she found herself picking at the rip with her nail. Kept her expression from being visible. "It's only natural that we would get a little closer."

"How close?" asked Keisha. Jamie continued picking at the plastic sleeve. "Oh, man, you slept with him, didn't you? When?"

"Since February."

"And you didn't tell me? What the hell, Jamie?"

"Because I knew you'd say, 'I told you so.'"

"I did tell you so. I knew the minute you told me you were going to work with him."

Jamie rolled her eyes. "I know. I know. He broke my heart. Crushed my soul to little pieces. Soured me on dreams. Believe me, I remember all about college. I didn't need reminding."

"You sure?"

"It was seven years ago. Things are—he's—different now. I'm different now too."

"I know—"

"Then stop implying I'm stupid." She already felt stupid enough.

Beside her, she could hear Keisha making agitated sniffing sounds. It was what she did when she was emotional. Made Jamie feel like a jerk for blowing up the way she did. "I'm sorry," she said. "Talking about Whit makes me super sensitive. I shouldn't have snapped at you."

"I'm sorry I kept bringing up college," Keisha replied. "I didn't mean to make you feel stupid. You should always feel like you can tell me anything."

Looking over, Jamie saw her friend's false eyelashes batting rapidly. She'd forgotten how emotional Keisha was likely to be feeling this week. "Are you going to cry?"

"No, I'm not."

"At least wait until I'm done," the makeup artist

chimed in. "God, weddings have so much drama. Who's this Whit person anyway?"

"Her ex-boyfriend," Keisha told him.

He jerked back the lipstick brush he was holding. "You're sleeping with your ex? Keep talking."

"It's not like you think. He's a very sweet person."

The man looked at Keisha, who nodded. "He is. The only reason I said anything, Jamie, is because I was worried about you. The last thing I want is to see you get hurt."

Her friend wasn't the only emotional one. Jamie blinked back a few tears of her own. "I know," she said. If there was one thing she could count on in this world, it was that Keisha had her back. Sisters forever. "I'm sorry I didn't tell you. I just wanted to keep everything in a private little bubble for a while, you know?"

"I get it," Keisha said. "When I met Terrance, I didn't want to share him with anyone either. Does this mean you two are a thing again?"

"Maybe?"

"You don't sound very certain."

Because she wasn't. The wedding was in a few days. Once it was over, Jamie wasn't sure what would happen. One second her heart was singing with happiness. The next her head was quoting Churchill. *"Those who fail to learn from history are condemned to repeat it."*

She didn't know which to listen to anymore. "We're kind of taking things one day at a time," she told Keisha.

Hence her hopes going down and up and back again. "Ahh…" Keisha said, "now you acting all bummed out makes sense. He hasn't said anything about how he feels?"

I want people to know how important you were to me. That's what he'd said. *Were important*, not *are important*, her head had immediately noted.

"He says a lot of things," she told Keisha. "But nothing specific. All I know is that after the wedding, there's no business excuse for us to keep seeing each other. I don't know if our relationship will continue or if I should prepare myself to say goodbye. That's why I'm bummed out."

"Have you talked with him?"

"About what? Us?" Jamie's heart practically went into arrhythmia at the suggestion. "No, I'm just going to play it cool and let things work out however they're supposed to."

Keisha pursed her newly mocha-colored lips. "In other words, you're going to do the exact same thing you did in college and let him think it's no big deal if he leaves."

"Why not?" Jamie asked back. "Whether he leaves or stays isn't going to change just because we talked about it. Why make the situation awkward if there's no need?"

"You said something similar back then too. Didn't stop your heart from breaking."

"My heart is better protected this time."

And then it hit her. For all her vacillating back and forth, her heart had beaten out her head. She wanted a future with Whit. Wanted to believe things would be different this time. If she never asked him, never knew otherwise, then she still had hope. Better to hope during uncertainty than be crushed with certainty.

She grabbed Kish's hand. "Look, your wedding is this weekend. We should be focused on you! There'll be plenty of time to dwell on my relationship issues when you get back from your honeymoon. Okay?"

"All right. If you're sure. I still think you should talk to him instead of letting him make the decision—again—but it you think it's better to play it cool, I won't say anything."

"Thank you." It was exactly what Jamie wanted.

"But," her friend waved a finger, "my original threat stands. You bring drama to my wedding, and I *will* kill you."

Whit sat perfectly still, his hands holding the ends of his enamel pen. His face was a blank mask. In fact, he looked so composed that a stranger walking by the foundation conference room might assume he was listening to an irate donor. They would never know his chest burned with agitation.

At the other end of the conference table, his grandfather ran a hand through his thick silver hair. "Aren't you going to say anything for yourself?"

"I'm not sure what you want me to say," he replied. "I'm not going to change my mind. I want people to know what happened."

"Good luck. I'll get an injunction. Make sure that piece of trash never sees the light of day."

"Go ahead," he told him. "Controversy makes for great publicity. Either way my story will get out. That's what matters to me. Letting people learn from my mistakes. Whether or not the book is published is secondary."

Whenever his grandfather got angry, there were two small bumps in the center of his forehead that would start to turn red. Currently, they were the color of crimson. Whit twisted the pen back and forth. The only surprise about his grandfather's appearance this morning was that he hadn't appeared sooner. Whit had been expecting him ever since his phone call back in February. The lack of communication these past three months had apparently been for him to "think things over."

"I cannot believe you would air your dirty laundry in some cheap tell-all," his grandfather was saying.

"Well-written." The man could insult him all he wanted, but he wasn't going to insult Jamie. "It's a well-written tell-all. In fact, I'd say it's very well-written."

"Regardless, it's a disgrace. Bad enough you traipsed all over Europe for years, but to tell people you were a drug addict? To accuse me of covering up an accident? What are you thinking?"

"Again, I'm only telling the truth." God, he wished he was seeing Jamie tonight instead of having to wait a whole twenty-four hours until the rehearsal dinner. Knowing he was seeing her sooner would have made this tirade a lot more bearable.

His grandfather shook his head. "And here I thought you were finally getting in line. I told your father he was too permissive with you." Whit nearly raised an eyebrow. Only his grandfather would call his parents' absentee parenting permissive.

"You realize that you'll never see a penny of my money, don't you? You'll be completely disowned. The money, this foundation, all of it will be gone."

"If that's the way you feel." He was forcing himself to sound unemotional to irritate his grandfather. On the inside, he felt like he'd been kicked. Losing the foundation he'd set up really hurt.

"Is there anything else?"

He grandfather didn't answer. His gaze went to the frames hanging on the wall, news reports highlighting the Martin charitable legacy before returning to Whit. They were cold and angry.

"Pack up your office and get out," he spat.

There was truly nothing left to say. Giving a nod, Whit took his leave.

Instead of returning to his office, however, he headed to the elevator. Cleaning out his office could wait while he got some fresh air.

The terrace looked a lot different than it did the night he and Jamie first visited. Tables and chairs were set up and there were flowers in the planters. Fortunately, the spring weather was still cool enough that the space didn't get that much use. He was, thankfully, alone.

The irony of his thought struck him, and he laughed. He'd always been alone. The only difference now was that his family had finally made it official. He wondered if his parents would care or if, in their "permissive" way, they'd be too busy with their latest artists' retreat to give his ostracism much thought.

Moving to the ledge, he looked down at the crowd of people walking back and forth. He never did get to count them. As he watched them and let his new reality settle in, he suddenly felt very alone.

Pulling out his cell, he autodialed Jamie's number. When she said hello, he felt the muscles in his shoulders relax.

"I called to say have fun tonight." The bridal party and a few college friends were taking Keisha out for a last single girls' night on the town. "Don't go too crazy. Remember, alcohol is not your friend. Take it from me, I'm an expert."

Her laugh was exactly the balm he needed. "You have my word—we'll keep the drunkenness to a minimum. We can't afford your level of debauchery anyhow. We'll probably spend our time dancing and keeping Terrance's sister from picking up random men."

What about men trying to pick Jamie up? The idea left a bitter taste in his mouth. "Just be careful," he said.

"Shouldn't I be the one warning you? You all are going to be gambling at the casino."

"We'll compromise then. You watch the champagne consumption and I'll keep the losses under a thousand."

"Deal." She paused. "Is everything all right? You sound weird. Are you outside?"

"I'm on the roof," he told her. "I had a meeting with Grandfather this morning."

"Oh."

"I have been officially excommunicated from the family. I'm to pack up my office and be out today."

"He fired you from the foundation too? But you're in charge."

"Can't run a family foundation if you're no longer part of the family."

She didn't need to say a word. Just the sound of her breathing was soothing enough. Closing his eyes, he imagined her hands upon his shoulder.

"How are you?" she asked finally. "You going to be okay?"

"I—I think so," he said. "I told you before, disinheritance doesn't really mean much to me. Since returning from Europe, I've invested my money well. I might not be a billionaire anymore, but what's one or two extra zeros on the bank account?"

She laughed.

"Losing the foundation sucks," he said. What started as atonement had become something that mattered to him. "But I'd already decided when my grandfather first issued his threat that I would establish my own foundation. I don't need the Martin family to be a philanthropist."

"No, you don't."

"They weren't much of a family anyway," he added. "At least now I don't have to wonder whether I mattered to them. The answer's pretty clear."

His offhand comment belied the heaviness in his stomach. He was surprised he felt anything, let alone sorrow. Then again, feeling alone was one thing. Knowing you were alone in the world was entirely another.

Except he wasn't alone, was he? He listened as the sound of Jamie's breathing mixed with the sound of the new age music she played while working.

"Is there anything I can do?" she asked.

"You are doing it. Just being able to tell someone has helped."

"I could cancel tonight if…"

"Don't." Not that it wasn't tempting, holing up in Jamie's bed rather than faking his way through Terrance's bachelor night, but he didn't want to be selfish. "Keisha would miss you if you weren't with her for her last hoorah. I'll be fine."

"If you're sure."

"Positive," he told her. "I'm meeting Terrance and the boys anyway. A few cigars, some poker and I'll be fine." Not really, but he would be eventually. In the meantime, he could smile his way through the night for Terrance's sake.

He kept her on the phone for another ten minutes, talking about nothing important, until Jamie had to take another call. Whit hung up with a promise to see her tomorrow night at the rehearsal dinner.

Just knowing he'd be with her in twenty-four hours made Whit feel so much better. Man, he was definitely hooked on her. Frighteningly so.

The smile faded from his face. What if he became too dependent on her? He'd already started seeking her out for emotional comfort. How long would it be until he couldn't live his life without her? Until he loved her?

Or was it already too late? He sat down at one of the wooden tables and thought of how much she'd come to mean in his life. What was he going to do when their love affair ended?

And why wouldn't it end? It was the intensity of the book project that had brought them together. Now without the project or the wedding, there was nothing keeping them tied to one another. Jamie had said the first night they were together in her hotel room that she wasn't looking for a lifelong commitment. Even if she was, why would she commit to someone as broken as him? Because of his money? Jamie wasn't like that; she never had been.

There had been a day in Madrid when he'd run out of painkillers and his source couldn't deliver until the next day. For twelve hours, Whit had curled up on his bed in the most excruciating pain of his life. His body had felt like it was on fire and he'd been convinced he was going to die.

Somehow, he had the feeling that if this kept going for much longer, Jamie leaving him would hurt far worse than that.

Maybe it'd be better if he walked away now.

The staff had opened the terrace windows for people to enjoy the view. As Jamie walked into the private dining room, she pulled her silk shawl tighter around her shoulders. Mid-May, the Boston temperatures weren't at summer level yet and the breeze off the Atlantic added to the chill. It wasn't only the air that had her feeling cold. She'd blame a sixth sense, if she had one. Something just didn't feel right.

"Rehearsal went well, don't you think?" a voice asked.

To her disappointment, it belonged to Jerome, the groomsman Keisha had assigned to walk her down the aisle. "A height thing," her friend had said.

He handed her a glass of white wine. "Keisha told me to give you this and to tell you it's pinot grigio."

"Thank you." Jamie smiled and took a sip. Glancing past his shoulder, she saw Whit talking to a pair of former classmates. He looked amazing in his blazer and sport shirt. Preppy casual.

She thought about joining him but didn't want to act clingy. After all, they weren't here as a couple, but as friends of mutual friends. She'd hoped Whit would think differently, but apparently not. It felt strange not being close to him. Over the past three months she'd grown used to feeling his hand resting on the small of her back or entwined with hers.

"I've got to say, Keisha looks a little rough around the edges still," Jerome remarked. "You ladies must have had quite a night."

"We definitely put a dent in Boston's liquor supply," Jamie replied. "Really, Keisha did. We made her do a shot every time she either mentioned Terrance or said the word *wedding*."

"I'm surprised she didn't get alcohol poisoning from it."

"So am I, now that I think about it."

Over in his group, someone said something to make Whit laugh. Again, Jamie got a strange feeling. He'd been laughing a lot, she noticed. Joking and reminiscing with his friends. Reminded her of when they were in college. No wonder her Spidey senses were tingling.

"Keisha said that you're a writer."

At Jerome's question, she turned her attention back to him and smiled. "Ghostwriter," she told him. "For the moment."

"I've always wondered what kind of people became ghostwriters. For some reason I pictured middle-aged white dudes smoking cigars in a back room."

"No cigars here," Jamie said.

"Or middle-aged white dudes," added Jerome.

What did it matter if Whit was laughing a lot? Any time you got a group of buddies together there would be joking around. This wasn't college. Whit wasn't alone and needing to hide behind his popularity anymore. He had her.

Do you have him though?

"I was wondering…"

With a mental apology, Jamie jerked her attention back to the man in front of her.

"I don't suppose you'd be willing to come and speak with my freshmen and sophomores, would you?" he asked. "I like to bring in guests to show them different careers that involve English and literature."

"I'd be glad to."

"Terrific." He pulled out his phone. "Let me get your contact info. I'll send you the details and we'll set something up."

While Jamie recited her email address, she saw Whit pat one of the men on the shoulder and head to the bar.

She smiled at Jerome. "If you'll excuse me, I need to go speak to someone before dinner."

After promising she would talk with him more

later in the evening, she made her way to the bar area as well. As she approached, butterflies took off in her stomach.

Oh, for crying out loud, she needed to stop this vacillating once and for all. Was she really planning to spend every minute she was with Whit waiting for the other shoe to drop? Would it be so difficult to believe she'd found something special?

It's okay to believe. That's what Whit had said. Maybe it was time to try again. After all, she had achieved some of those childhood dreams. She'd gotten the scholarship to the prestigious university, she was a published author—maybe not the kind she'd always envisioned but published nonetheless—and she was working on her great American novel. Why couldn't Prince Charming finally be hers too?

Whit was leaning against the wall, drinking a soda water. When he saw her, his face lit up for a moment before disappearing behind his glass.

She slipped herself into the space beside him. "Hey, stranger. Long time no see."

"Hey," he replied.

"Everything okay?" She was fine with playing things low-key, but she expected his response to be at least a little effusive.

"Sorry," he said. "Last night's lousy sleep is catching up to me."

"Only lack of sleep?" Yesterday had been a

traumatic day. While he'd tried to sound matter of fact on the phone, she knew his grandfather's dismissal must have hurt. "If you want to talk about what happened yesterday…"

"Not really." He quickly corrected his curtness. "I mean, this isn't the best time."

"I understand." Up close, she noticed there were fatigue lines around his mouth. If he took off his glasses, she bet she'd see circles under his eyes too. Their prominence was why she pushed aside her anxiety. He looked exhausted.

"How was last night?" she asked. "Did you all have fun?"

He shrugged. "It was standard bachelor night fare. We hit up the cigar shop, Terrance had too much whiskey and made stupid bets. He's going to have some answering to do when he gets back from his honeymoon."

"If he gets into too much trouble, I can help. We've got a few embarrassing photos from last night I'm sure Keisha wouldn't want him to see."

"I'll let him know," he said with a chuckle.

One of the things she'd always appreciated about Whit was how easily he could make conversation. She'd seen him meet complete strangers and within five minutes have them chatting away like they were old friends. Yet tonight the two of them couldn't do better than this stilted conversation. Why? "Are you sure you're all right?" she asked again.

"I told you, I'm fine. Please stop asking."

She flinched and he immediately shook his head. "I'm sorry. I didn't mean to snap. I've been doing a lot of socializing and I'm tired."

"You're forgiven," she said, "but only because I can see that you're wiped." Forgetting all about not acting clingy, she rose on tiptoes and rested her chin on his shoulder. "I'm sorry I can't stay and help you sleep. Bridesmaid's sleepover at Keisha's."

Whit touched her cheek. For the first time all day, his eyes drank her in, their blue color vivid and deep. Jamie's knees buckled. She wondered if there would ever be a time when she didn't fall into his gaze.

"I'll miss you." The fatigue made his voice oddly serious.

"It's only for tonight," she told him. "I'll make it up to you tomorrow."

"Actually, I…"

He was interrupted by the sound of glass tinkling. Terrance was tapping a fork against his wine goblet. "They're going to start serving dinner, so if everyone would please sit down."

"With your ceremony partner," Keisha added.

Whit's hand fell away from her cheek.

"I better go join Jerome," Jamie told him. At

the moment she hated Keisha for keeping them apart during the meal. "I'll miss you."

"Jams?" Before she could walk too far, Whit caught her wrist. "Can we talk after dinner?"

He had an abnormally serious look on his face. One that made her nerves jangle. "Of course you can," she told him. "There's no need to ask."

Between the different courses and all the toasts, dinner took forever. Jamie spent most of it chatting with Jerome about teaching literature to fifteen-year-olds. He was an entertaining dinner partner and his stories made her laugh. Unfortunately, she only half listened. Her mind was focused on Whit. What was so serious that he needed to speak with her tonight?

He's breaking up with you.

No. Her heart refused to listen to her negativity. Until Whit said the words himself, her heart was going to believe in the two of them.

Finally, they were serving the raspberry crisp. Keisha and Terrance had debated over the dessert choice for a week. Looked like Keisha won. She and Jerome laughed over the image of Keisha and Terrance locked in a battle royal between Fudgsicle cake and raspberry crisp.

Across the room, Whit stood up and excused himself. Jamie waited a respectable amount of time, then excused herself as well. She found him coming around the corner near the bathrooms.

"They're almost finished," she told him. "Do you want to talk now before Keisha drags me off?"

"Sure. Yeah." The answer didn't sound like his usual decisive self. "There's a bench at the other end of the corridor. Why don't we sit there? That way we won't be interrupted."

The butterflies were back in her stomach. "You're being awfully formal for a man who said nothing was wrong," she said. When they finally did sit down, she moved to sit close to him only to find he'd placed his hand on the space between them. She had to settle for sitting with her hand wrapped around his forearm. "What is it, Whit?"

"I'm sorry to drag you away for this conversation tonight, but this was too important to wait."

Jamie waited as he took a deep breath. By this time the butterflies were bouncing all over the place.

"I'm going to Italy," he said.

"Oh." That wasn't the news she'd expected.

Whit, his eyes focused on a spot in the distance, continued. His voice was flat, as if spitting out prewritten words. "I thought writing the book would give me closure, but it didn't. I still think about what happened all the time."

"I'm not surprised. You said yourself you would never completely forget about it."

"I know, but I realized the other night that I won't truly get closure until I talk with Bianca's family and apologize. Both for what happened and for what my grandfather did. That's the only way I'll truly be able to move on."

Shameful as it was, Jamie felt a wave of relief. She'd let her insecurity get the better of her—again—when all Whit wanted was to make things right with the DeLucas.

She wondered if he'd come to this conclusion because of the fight with his grandfather. Didn't matter either way, but she could see how ending the ties with his family might spur him on to make things right with another.

Now his odd behavior tonight made sense. This couldn't have been an easy decision. If he thought apologizing to Bianca's family would help him come to terms with his guilt, however, then that's what he should do. In fact, she'd gladly go with him for support.

Already thinking of how she could clear her schedule, she asked him, "When are you thinking of leaving?"

"I'm flying out tomorrow night, straight after the wedding."

"Tomorrow," she repeated flatly. That's why he'd wanted to talk with her tonight.

"I didn't want to blindside you with the news at the wedding."

Jamie looked down at her hand on his arm. She hadn't realized, but she was gripping his jacket tightly. "I didn't realize you were leaving so quickly."

"I want to leave as soon as possible. The longer I wait, the more chance I'll lose my nerve."

She guessed that made sense. It all felt very sudden to her, but she wasn't the one who needed to make the trip. "When are you coming back?"

The longer he didn't answer, the more Jamie's chest began to squeeze. Slowly, he turned to look at her. Regret filled his face. "I don't know. Not for a while."

Jamie thought she was going to be sick. Whit was leaving her again. How many times had she warned herself that this was going to happen? She *knew*, damn it. She knew when he started referring to their relationship in the past tense. But despite everything, her stupid heart still wanted to hope. Still clung to the fantasy that this time would be different. What an idiot. Thinking that this time, Whit would fall in love with her? When was she going to learn that she wasn't what he wanted? She was just someone he'd needed briefly, in the moment.

Well, he would not get the satisfaction of seeing her fall apart. She refused to let him see her heart breaking in two.

"I appreciate the advance notice," she said. To her amazement, her voice didn't crack. "Tomorrow is going to be crazy as it is, without trying to have a private conversation."

"I appreciate you understanding."

She understood all right. Understood so much it hurt. "I hope you find the closure you're looking for, Whit. You're too good a man to carry so much guilt around forever."

Why was he looking at her like he'd expected her to say more? She was having a difficult enough time getting these words out without choking. "It's been a wonderful three months. Thank you."

An emotion flickered across his face, but she refused to analyze it. Summoning up the last of her courage, she kissed his cheek. "I'd better get back to the dining room. Keisha's going to be in full Bridezilla mode until after the ceremony. I'll see you tomorrow."

It took everything she had, but she managed to walk away from him without breaking into a run.

"Goodbye, Jams." Whit whispered the words as he watched her walk slowly away from him. He'd done it. He'd broken things off with Jamie while he could still stomach losing her.

Someone needed to clue his body in, though, because his chest felt like it was being cracked open.

Thanks for a wonderful three months. Three months of the most incredible emotional connection of his life, and that was how she reacted to it ending. Same calm, collected voice as seven years ago. The voice that had kept him from suggesting they try to continue the relationship long distance.

A part of him wanted to run after her and fight. Make her see how much she meant to him. The smarter half knew better. If she hadn't fallen in love with him seven years ago, when he'd been on top of the world, what made him think she'd fall in love with him now?

He just wished he hadn't fallen so hard for her this second time. For three amazing months, Jamie had banished his loneliness and his self-loathing and in return, he'd given her his heart.

Face it, Martin. No one who matters ever wants you around. Tomorrow he would board a plane for Italy. What he'd told Jamie was the truth; he did want to track down the DeLucas. Until he spoke with them, he wouldn't truly have closure. It was only the reason for his hasty departure that he kept to himself.

"Hey, Whit!" Terrance hollered from the dining room doorway. "We're heading down to the lobby bar for a nightcap. You in?"

"Be right there." Whit wiped at his eyes with his thumb. His heartache would have to wait until his flight tomorrow night. Until then, it was time to pretend he was happy.

Jamie had to give herself credit. Not only did she make it back to the dining room without crying, but she made it through the bridal sleepover. Only when everyone had said good-night and she was sharing the guest bed with Terrance's sister did she shed silent tears.

In the morning, she blamed her puffy eyes on a lack of sleep, and, at Keisha's orders, covered them with a cold compress. Today was her best friend's wedding day, and she'd promised Keisha there would be no drama.

Her friend deserved nothing but positive energy. It wasn't her fault Jamie had ignored all her warnings. And so she laughed with the other girls as they got their hair and makeup done, teased Keisha when she couldn't hook up her strapless bodysuit, and cheered when they had one final champagne toast.

Everything went fine, until they reached the church and she saw Whit.

The sighting was by accident. Keisha asked her to peek inside and tell her if the flowers looked like her photo sample. When she looked through the door, Terrance and his entourage were already standing at the front of the church. Immediately, her eyes went to Whit. Even as a supporting player in a wedding, his was the presence commanding attention. Jamie started to tremble. How was she going to handle seeing him every time she turned around?

"How do they look?" Keisha whispered. "Did she use the yellow roses?"

"She did." Jamie cleared her throat. "They look great."

So did Keisha. She was dressed in a white trumpet-shaped gown unembellished except for a gold-and-crystal ribbon. Her dark hair had been pulled into a puff while her veil, held in place by a comb, flowed down her back. Jamie's eyes grew damp. At that moment she both loved and envied her best friend. Keisha was about to marry the love of her life. No matter how badly her heart hurt, Jamie would do her best to not mess up this moment for her.

"You look like a princess," she told Keisha with a watery smile.

"I know," Keisha replied. The joke broke some of the nervous tension. "Now get in line. I spent a lot of time planning this order."

The ceremony was beautiful. It was difficult, but Jamie managed to keep her eyes on the happy couple instead of staring at Whit for most of the ceremony. Terrance and Keisha had written their own vows. When it was Keisha's turn, she pulled out a white slip of paper, cleared her throat and began to read.

"What is love? Is it the tremor of a heart at first sight? Or a flower that blooms larger every spring?"

Jamie's eyes shot to Whit. He looked at her.

"Or a river whose waters flow endlessly into the sea? Love is all of these and more. Love is a best friend, a companion, a soul mate, a consoler, a guide. Love forgives and is forgiven. Love never dies."

As Keisha read, Jamie looked at Whit and silently repeated the words to him. She could feel the tears running down her cheeks. She didn't care. She was telling Whit how she felt. When Keisha was finished, she smiled at him.

Whit looked away.

After that, it was all she could do to get through the rest of the ceremony.

"Wow," Jerome remarked as he escorted her out of the church. "Keisha's poem really struck you, didn't it?"

Ran over her like a Mack truck was more like it.

As soon as the photographs were finished, she ran straight for the ladies' room. Tossing her bouquet on the vanity counter, she stared at her reflection. "Stupid, stupid idiot," she hissed.

This was what happened when you let yourself dream. As soon as you started to think maybe you could have Prince Charming and the happy ending, you got smacked back down to reality with a reminder that you weren't good enough for him.

Why did Whit have to tell her all that stuff about her deserving her dreams in the first place? Was it some kind of joke? Some sick way of getting her hopes up before crushing her once and for all, or was he just a stupid, insensitive idiot?

"Damn you, Whit Martin!" She pounded her fist on the lounge area vanity table, cursing his name until all the emotion she'd been holding in since last night choked its way out. Pressing her palms to the counter surface, her body shuddered with deep, tearless sobs.

"What the…?"

At the sound of Keisha's voice, Jamie stood up and reached for a tissue to find Keisha and the rest of the wedding party in the doorway staring at her.

"I think we need a minute," Keisha said to the other women. "Can you wait outside?"

"Sorry," Jamie said once the two of them were alone. "I was a little verklempt at the ceremony and needed a moment."

Her friend folded her arms. "My wedding made you break down in hysterical crying?"

"Why not? Sisters for life, remember?"

"Sisters don't lie to each other, so spill it." Gathering her veil in her arms, Keisha perched herself on the edge of the vanity. "What did Whit do now?"

"Nothing. Turn around and I'll unpin your veil."

"Fine," Keisha said, doing as she asked. "But you still have to tell me."

"I can't. I promised you there'd be no drama."

"Sweetie, the drama boat sailed as soon as we found you doubled over sobbing in the bathroom. I take it he broke up with you."

Jamie began folding the tulle in half and then quarters. "He's going back to Europe. Indefinitely. I can't believe I was stupid enough to fall for him twice. What's worse, I knew! I even said, if he didn't fall in love with me last time, he wasn't going to suddenly fall in love this time around.

"I feel like a pathetic idiot," she muttered.

"You're not an idiot," Keisha told her.

"Not funny."

"Okay, you're not pathetic either. You've got a blind spot. We all have some guy that we're so crazy for that we go a little nuts."

"Let me guess, yours is Terrance." Jamie handed over the veil. "Newsflash: you can be as crazy in love as you want when they love you back. You know what the most confusing part is?"

she asked. "I didn't initiate any of it. He was the one who kissed me first." The one who'd said he needed her. "Why would he do all those romantic things if he didn't care?"

"I don't know, honey. Maybe he's just a jerk."

Jamie shook her head. "No. I spent three months interviewing him, and he's not a jerk. Underneath everything, he's a sweet, lonely man."

"Then maybe he's wicked confused. Some guys don't know a good thing when they see it."

"Hey, Keisha!" One of the bridesmaids poked her head through the door. "Terrance is looking for you."

"I better go see what my husband wants. Man, that sounds so cool, doesn't it?" She gave a little shimmy at the end that made Jamie laugh. "Are you going to be okay?"

"I'll be fine. I'm sorry I spoiled your wedding."

"You didn't spoil anything," Keisha assured her. "Although the best revenge is to enjoy yourself. Why don't you fix your makeup and join us on the dance floor?"

Keisha was right, Jamie thought. She could either stay in here and cry all day, or she could go back out and let Whit and the rest of the world think she didn't have a broken heart.

"They'll be plenty of time to cry later," Jamie agreed. She grabbed another tissue.

* * *

Whit watched the bartender mixing cosmopolitans. The woman added a generous helping of vodka to the other ingredients before shaking them together and filling three martini glasses with the red liquid. His mouth watered a little.

Behind him, the green grounds of a botanical garden rolled out where the reception was in full swing. Over the sounds of the jazz quartet, you could hear peals of laughter as guests mingled in the yard.

"How good are you with a vodka martini?" he asked the woman.

"Very good," she replied. "You want one?"

He wanted more than one. A good buzz was exactly what he needed to take away the ache in his chest. It had been pure hell seeing Jamie in the church. She looked beautiful in green. When she walked down the aisle, everyone else in the church had disappeared. The minister. Terrance. Keisha. He only had eyes for Jamie, and it hurt like hell to look. It was going to take a long time before he forgot the image of her when Keisha had read her vows. When he first noticed her looking in his direction and saw the tears, he'd thought... But any fool could see that her attention was on the bride and groom. A few drinks would dim the picture until he boarded the plane. Then a few more in the air would tide him over until Italy.

Making everything he'd worked for the past two years meaningless. No matter how lonely he felt, he wouldn't go backwards.

"Changed my mind," he told the bartender. "Club soda with lime, please."

Jamie would be proud of him, he thought with more than a little irony.

He tossed a tip in the bartender's jar and went looking for a seat. Sooner or later, he'd join up with the guys from college for another round of reminiscing, but at the moment he just wanted a quiet corner. Under the circumstances, being jovial took work. Last night's fun had exhausted him. Halfway through the evening, he'd realized that while he counted all of these people as good friends, none of them really knew who he was. The person they knew was a superficial version of himself, a carefree role he played because he didn't know who he was either. The only person who knew him, really knew him, was Jamie. She was the only person he'd let close enough to find out. That'd show him, wouldn't it?

He settled for returning to the head table, where he found a piece of chocolate wedding cake laid out on a napkin. His friends were on the dance floor with their dates, swaying uncoordinatedly to the syncopated rhythms.

Through the crowd, he could see Jamie dancing with Jerome on the far end of the dance floor.

From the looks of it, the man was attempting to teach her a dance move, but for whatever reason, the lesson wasn't clicking. Every time Jamie messed up, she would cover her lips and giggle. They looked like they were having a fine time.

Whit wanted to kill them both.

"Dude, shouldn't you be on the dance floor leading everyone?" Wearing the same goofy grin he'd been wearing for hours, Terrance plopped down in the chair next to him. His bowtie was undone along with the top two buttons of his tuxedo shirt.

"Someone should have told me weddings were this exhausting," he said. "Every time I turn around, someone's taking a picture of me or I'm being dragged over to talk to someone. Keisha better not be planning on a big wedding night because I'm out the minute my head hits the pillow."

He picked up Whit's cup and took a drink. "How you doing with all the alcohol and stuff?"

"You don't have to keep asking, you know," Whit replied. His friend had been checking in ever since the end of the bachelor party when Whit had finally told him he was in recovery.

"I know, but I want to make sure. Man, I still can't believe you didn't tell me before. We're friends."

"I didn't tell anyone. I was…" Embarrassed and ashamed. "I didn't want anyone to know how bad things had gotten. I thought you might not want me around if you did."

"Why the hell would you think that?" His friend gave him a smack between the shoulder blades. "Did the pills kill your brain cells or something? You don't bail on the people you care about."

He'd said something similar at the bachelor party. When Whit told him about Bianca and his addiction battles, he fully expecting his friend to be disgusted. Instead, the man immediately pledged to support Whit in whatever way he needed. It was the second time someone didn't hate him for his crimes.

"I know," he replied, as a different kind of shame washed over him. One caused by not trusting in his friends' loyalty.

"You better." His friend slung an arm around his shoulders. "So, are you cool?"

"Yeah, I'm fine." His moment of weakness from before had been just that: a moment. No matter how miserable he felt, he wouldn't derail his sobriety.

"Good to hear. Jamie looks like she's having a good time."

Whit's eyes traveled back to the dance floor, where Jerome had changed his position. Standing behind Jamie, he had his hands on her hips and was moving their pelvises together.

"Doesn't she though?" he said through gritted teeth.

"How come you're not out there with her? Aren't you into her anymore? You were all over each other at college."

"It's complicated," Whit replied. Better than saying, *She doesn't care that I'm leaving town.* He glared at the couple on the dance floor. Did Jamie know he had a clear view of their antics? Was that Jerome's hand sliding up her rib cage?

That's it. The English teacher was toast. He pushed his chair back with a growl.

"You!" A whirlwind in white appeared in his face. Keisha scowled at him. "I have been looking for you all day. All I asked is that no one bring drama to our wedding because Terrance and I have better things to do than deal with you all's stuff. What did you go and do now? You go and break my best friend's heart at the rehearsal dinner. Boy, you are so lucky I don't kick your billionaire behind."

Terrance looked back and forth between the two of them. "Wait a second. You and Jamie were a thing again? How did I not know this?"

"It was only for a few months, and we kept things low-key," Whit said while he stepped back from Keisha.

"And you dumped her at the rehearsal dinner? Man, that's cold."

"I didn't dump her. I'm leaving for Italy tonight and don't know when I'll be back." Why was he being labeled the bad guy in this? "Anyway, I don't know what you think you heard, but I didn't break anyone's heart. Jamie was fine with me going." She'd barely blinked, if he recalled. "She told me herself she wasn't looking for a lifetime commitment."

"Puh-lease." Keisha waved the comment away. "She said the same thing last time you guys hooked up too. She didn't mean it then either."

"What?"

"She knew you were leaving for Europe and she didn't want to seem clingy or stand in your way. Wasn't until after you left that she fell apart."

Whit's pulse started to quicken. Was Keisha saying that Jamie... That she... "Why would she fall apart?" He whispered the question.

"Why do you think, you idiot. She was totally nuts about you. Still is."

"But she said..."

"She says a lot of things," Keisha told him with a roll of her eyes. "Trust me, she's crazy about you and you treated her like dirt."

Whit groped behind him until he found a chair. "But I thought... God, I'm such an idiot," he said, washing a hand over his face.

"Good Lord," Keisha said. "Did you two ever talk?"

"We talked all the time." Just not about this.

A mistake he was going to rectify right now.

Dance moves were a lot easier to learn when you were actually in a good mood. Pretending to be happy required paying attention. Was this what it had been like for Whit all those years?

Jerome twirled her around and she pushed Whit's name out of her head. She wasn't going to think about him, nor was she going to look across the dance floor at where he was sitting. Instead, she let Jerome catch her waist from behind and teach her how to grind. "Uh-oh," she heard Jerome say. "Someone looks angry."

Glancing to her left, she saw Whit bearing down on them. Jerome was right. He did look upset.

He stood in front of her. "You and I need to talk."

"No," she replied curtly. Who did he think he was, interrupting her on the dance floor and expecting her to jump when he said so? He'd broken up with her. She wasn't going to be a patsy for him anymore. "Well, it'll have to wait. I'm dancing with Jerome."

Whit leaned in to whisper in her ear. "It wasn't a request." The predatory gleam in his eyes sent an embarrassingly needy shiver down her back.

Before she could say a word, however, Jerome

decided to wedge himself between them. "The lady said she was dancing."

"It's all right, Jerome. I don't mind," Jamie said. "I'm sure...eep!" Whit grabbed her hand and led her away before she could finish what she was saying.

CHAPTER ELEVEN

"Was that really necessary?" she demanded.

Whit didn't answer. He led her outside and down the walkway until they reached a Japanese lantern garden on the edge of the property. There was a giant concrete lantern in the center of a floral circle. Whit gestured for Jamie to stand by the figure while he rested his hand on one of its curved prongs. As a result, she found herself looking up into his blue, very dark blue, eyes.

"Were you in love with me in college?" he asked bluntly.

What the—? "Who told you that?" she choked out.

"You know who told me."

Keisha.

"Is it true?" he pressed.

"We're talking about seven years ago. What difference does it make now?" She ducked under his arm and walked to the other side of the garden. The afternoon sun was low in the sky, casting them in shadows. Jamie shivered at the chill. "Don't you have a plane to catch?" she asked, rubbing her arms.

"Then Keisha was telling the truth. Why didn't you tell me?"

Was he kidding? "What good would telling you have done? You were heading to Europe anyway. From the very beginning you told me you were leaving and that you weren't looking for a serious relationship."

"You said you weren't either."

"I had no choice!" she snapped. "Would you have dated me if I had said I'd spent two years just hoping you'd notice me?" Whit looked at the ground. "That's what I thought."

"So, yes, stupid me, I said I wasn't looking for a relationship, when I really wanted you to fall in love with me. And then you left for Europe and I cried my eyes out every single day for a month."

She was angry now. Angry enough for hot tears to start spilling onto her cheeks. Damn Keisha. Why did she have to tell him anything?

Well, if he was going to know, then he was going to know everything. "You want to know why I stopped writing my novel? Why I stopped believing all my dreams could come true? Because of you." She swiped at the tears with the back of her hand. "Because when you left, I realized stupid romantic fantasies don't ever come true, so why bother reaching for them."

Out of breath, she stood in front of the azalea bushes with her fists clenched, her chest heaving from exertion. "Then you had to come back and make me believe all over again, only to step on them for a second time."

The color had drained from Whit's face. He looked like he'd been slapped. Good, thought Jamie. That's what she'd meant to do.

He ran a hand across his lips. "But when I told you I was going to Italy yesterday, you didn't—"

"Break down and go crazy? Excuse me for trying to preserve a little pride."

What a mess. Her nose was running, and her cheeks were streaked with tears. All she wanted was to go home, pull the covers over her head and cry for the next thirty-six hours. "If you're satisfied, I'd like to go to the conservatory now." She turned her back on him.

"I was scared."

Standing at the garden's edge, Jamie looked over her shoulder. Whit stood under the Japanese maple, looking at her from under heavy lids. "I was scared," he repeated. "I knew it was only a matter of time before you left me and…"

"And what?" she asked, slowly turning around.

"I've never felt like this with anyone else. I spent so many years just floating along, trying not to think about how lonely I was."

He looked her in the eye. "These past three months, I've forgotten what loneliness felt like. I've been so happy. Happier than I've ever been."

"Then why leave?" she asked. If he was so happy, why take off for Italy?

"Call it a preemptive strike. The first night we were together you told me you weren't looking for a lifetime commitment."

Jamie pressed a fist to her stomach, memories of that night coming back to her. His hesitancy. Her reassuring him that she wasn't looking for more than just his touch. "So you decided to leave me because of that?" Surely one small comment couldn't carry that much weight?

"Why wouldn't I? A person tells you the same thing twice, you figure they really mean it."

"I already told you why I said that to you in college. You were notorious for only having short-term hookups. I didn't want you to think I expected more than that."

"The first night, fine, but you acted casual the entire time we were together."

"Because I didn't want you to think I was clingy."

"Seriously?" His face scrunched in that adorable way he had when confused. "It didn't dawn on you though, after all those months together, that I might be okay with clingy?"

"I don't know," Jamie said. Her eyes were tearing up again. Probably from the lump jammed in the back of her throat. "You were… I never thought I had a chance with you to begin with."

"A semester and a half, Jams. I'd never spent more than a weekend with a girl. How could you not know you were special?"

Did he want a list? How about because she'd seen him as the most perfect boy in the world while she was just a nerdy scholarship girl? Or that he'd told her from day one that he was going to Europe after graduation?

Swiping at the tears on her cheeks, she decided to jump right to the top of the list. "Because you never told me. You would tell me I was 'awesome' or that I never bored you, but you never said I was special or that you cared about me."

She watched while he absorbed her words. Behind his glasses, his blue eyes widened with realization, only to turn cloudy again. "Neither did you," he said.

"I didn't want to scare you off."

The air between them felt remarkably heavy. Jamie would have thought the opposite after finally saying everything she'd been holding inside since college. Instead, her nerves remained tense. Whit had turned to the statue. Palms pressed against the cement, he slowly shook his head back and forth.

"I thought…" she heard him start. "At graduation, you were so cool with my leaving. You told me to have a nice life. That's why I decided not to suggest…"

"Suggest what?" she asked.

"That we keep things going while I was away."

Jamie's breath stuck in her chest. "Wait, you were going to…" He'd wanted to…?

She started to laugh. It was either that or cry, and she was already crying. Tears streaked her cheeks.

"Jamie?"

Whit had crossed the space between them to grasp her by the shoulders. "Are you all right?" he asked, eyes filled with confusion and concern.

"God, we're both idiots," she said. "The two of us were so afraid of rejection, we created our own self-fulfilling prophecy." If they'd only talked, really talked, they could have saved themselves years of heartache.

And they'd nearly made the same mistake all over again.

She sniffed. "All these years I thought you didn't want me."

"Same here," he said with a crooked smile. "Especially this time. What kind of woman would want to stay with someone as broken as me?"

"I would." Somehow, Whit's hands had found their way to her cheeks. As he brushed away her tears with his thumbs, Jamie let herself lean into his touch. "Maybe we both have a few things to learn about communication," she said.

"And trust," he added.

Cradling her face, he turned her face to his. Jamie had always said looking into Whit's eyes made her feel like she was falling through a cloudless sky. Looking into them now, to find never-ending emotion shimmering in their depths, it felt more like soaring.

"I love you, Jamie," he said. "I think a part of me has always loved you, or knew I could, but I was too young and scared and stupid to realize." His hand was trembling as he brushed his fingers across her lips. Jamie sucked in her breath. "I know I blew it with you last night, but if you give me a second chance, I'll never let you doubt my feelings for you again."

Jamie wanted to say yes. Oh, how she wanted to say yes. "What about Italy and wanting to find Bianca's family?" she asked. Was any of the story true?

"I wasn't lying about Italy. I still need to go if my conscience is ever going to find peace."

In other words, he was still leaving. Jamie's shoulders dropped.

"But I don't want to go without you by my side." He took her hands in his. "Please tell me you'll give me a second chance?"

"Technically, this is your third chance," she teased. "And I love you too. The real you. Not the fantasy golden boy from college, but the broken, flawed, beautiful man standing here before me. I love you more than you can imagine."

Whit's face lit up like a man who'd won an amazing prize, only the prize was her. Pulling her into his arms, he brushed the dampness from her cheeks. "I love you," he whispered. "I love you. I love you. I love you." Marking each declaration with a featherlight kiss.

The moment was so perfect Jamie nearly cried. She couldn't believe what was happening. Whit Martin loved her and wanted to take her away with him. And when Whit finally kissed her sweet and slow, the moment was everything she'd ever dreamed of and more.

Keisha stood on the bandstand and waved her bouquet. In front of her waited a large percentage of her female guests. "Okay, ladies. Everyone needs to play fair. I don't want to see any hair pulling or eye gouging out there. It's only a bunch of flowers."

Standing on the edge of the dance floor, Jamie shook her head at her friend's theatrics. "Sometimes I think she should have gone on the stage instead of studying microbiology," she said to the man on whose chest she was currently resting her head.

"She definitely has a flair for the dramatic, doesn't she?" Whit replied.

"Hey, no drama at the wedding, remember?"

His strong arms tightened around her waist. She'd been floating on a cloud since their talk in the Japanese garden and she hoped she never came down again.

"I canceled my flight," Whit told her, "and booked a hotel room for the night."

She looked up at him. "Is that an invitation?"

"I don't know. Is that an acceptance?"

Jamie answered with a kiss.

Meanwhile, up on stage, Keisha continued rounding up the guests. "Do I have all the single ladies on the dance floor? Doesn't matter how old you are. You're still eligible." Keisha's grandmother and great aunt jogged out to join the circle.

"Remind me again what the big deal is about catching the bouquet?" Whit asked her.

"Supposedly the woman who catches the bouquet at the wedding will be the next one to get married."

"Jamie Rutkowski," Keisha called her out. "You're not married yet. Get your sweet self out on the floor."

Whit kissed her on top of her head. "You better go. You know she won't give up until you're out there."

"I know. I'll be right back." With a reluctant sigh, Jamie pulled herself away from Whit's arms and started toward the center of the dance floor.

"On the count of three," Keisha called. "One."

"Hey, Jams, wait a second." Jogging up behind her, Whit leaned down to whisper in her ear. "Why don't you go ahead and catch that bouquet?"

"Two."

Jamie turned and stared at him. Whit smiled at her like she was the only woman on the dance floor...

"Three!"

And a bouquet of yellow roses landed right in her arms.

EPILOGUE

THE CEMETERY IN Bergamon resembled an open-air museum. Large statues, both religious and non-religious, rose toward the sky in a tribute to the people buried below. It was a beautiful, peaceful place to rest for eternity.

As well as to say one final apology.

Jamie's sandals made a soft padding sound as she walked past tourists to the center of the cemetery. Whit stood before a white marble cross. Surprisingly simple in comparison to the more ornate monuments, it bore the name Bianca De-Luca. A small bouquet of flowers, bought at the open-air market that morning, lay at the base.

"Right where her parents said it would be," she said as she slipped her hand into his.

"They gave good directions," he replied.

Once they'd gotten to Italy, they'd had a productive ten days. After a brief search, they'd located the DeLucas in Rome. Mr. and Mrs. De-Luca had been told that no one knew how their daughter managed to overdose while on the boat and that she died alone. When they'd learned the truth, they were justifiably angry. Mr. DeLuca had spent several minutes cursing Whit's family for lying to protect Whit.

Whit showed so much strength during the visit. He sat and let Bianca's father hurl verbal abuse in his direction, his face flinching with each word the man spat. Jamie hurt for him. After several minutes, Mr. DeLuca tired.

"Mi dispiace," Whit said then. "I'm sorry. I would have stopped my grandfather if I had known."

Mrs. DeLuca took his hands. "I believe you," she said. "I'm glad we know the truth. Now we know Bianca wasn't alone."

Whit blinked back tears. "I wish I had done more to try and save her."

"You would have only postponed the inevitable. Our daughter was lost to drugs for a long time. It was only a matter of time before we got the phone call."

"You want to honor our daughter's memory?" asked Mr. DeLuca. "Don't waste your second chance."

"I won't," Whit vowed. He looked at Jamie, and her heart nearly burst from the love she saw in his eyes. "I promise."

After their visit to the DeLucas, they went to Capri, where Whit convinced the authorities to let him read Bianca's autopsy report. There were so many different intoxicants in Bianca's system that the cocktail had caused her to go into cardiac arrest. While they would never know for sure, it was possible she'd died even as Whit was bent over the rail being sick. Jamie knew that would make little difference to Whit. A part of him would always remember and regret what had happened. But knowing the whole story, together with the DeLucas' forgiveness, was finally helping Whit forgive himself and achieve the closure he'd been looking for.

She'd been right: there was a bidding war for Whit's memoir. *Polo Junkie* sold to a New York publishing house for seven figures. Naturally, Whit's grandfather threatened to get an injunction, but after a cabal of Martin lawyers warned it could cause even more controversy, backed down from the threat. Just as he said he would, Whit used the money to fund several substance abuse charities.

As for Jamie, the auction boosted her value and demand as a ghostwriter. She was flattered, but far too busy with her own novel to take on any new projects. Her agent, having read the opening chapters, wholeheartedly agreed.

In between their fact-finding had been nights of holding one another and whispering promises. When they left the cemetery, Whit told her, he planned to give her a proper European tour, including tracking down Camelot in England. Jamie almost told him she had found her Camelot already, but he'd been so excited to plan the trip for her that she didn't.

Back at the gravesite, she nodded at the flowers. "They look nice. I'm sure she appreciates them."

"I hope so," Whit said.

"Does it help? Getting to say goodbye?"

"A little. I told her I would do my best to make sure others don't fall down the same rabbit hole she and I did."

"You're going to do a lot of good," she told him. He'd already started the groundwork for a new foundation. The firing of the man behind the mission hadn't sat well with his former staff, and most had already defected to Whit's new venture from the Martin one.

Whit let out a long breath. "Would it be weird if I said I loved you in the middle of the cemetery?"

"No weirder than the other zillion times you've said it on this trip," she said.

"Good, because I have seven years to make up for. I refuse to let another day go by without telling you how glad I am to have you back."

Jamie would never get tired of telling him too. Slowly but surely, they were learning to say what was in their hearts. "I love you, Mr. Martin," she said.

"And I..." He lifted her hand. The gold band

he'd placed on her finger a few days earlier glistened in the afternoon sun. "I love you, Mrs. Martin. What do you say, shall we go start our future?"

* * * * *

*If you enjoyed this story,
check out these other great reads from
Barbara Wallace*

**A Year with the Millionaire Next Door
Her Convenient Christmas Date
One Night in Provence
Their Christmas Miracle**

All available now!